"I'm pregnant."

For a few seconds he said nothing, seconds that stretched like hours for Devon. She was shivering with nerves. Then he said, each word falling like a stone, "Who's the father?"

"You are. Of course."

"Of course?" he said silkily. "I don't know the first thing about you—you could be sleeping with a dozen other men."

Appalled, she gaped at him. "There aren't any other men, and do you think I *want* to be pregnant by you? That I'm trying to trap you into marriage? Believe me, you're the last man on earth I'd ever want to marry."

He closed the gap between them. Devon fought for breath. "So what are you going to do?" he said with icy precision.

"I'm going to keep it, Jared. I'll manage."

"Yes, you will. Because you'll be my wife."

Legally wed,
But he's never said…
"I love you."
They're…

Wedlocked!

The series where marriages are made
in haste…and love comes later….

Look out for the next book in the WEDLOCKED!
miniseries next month:

Wife: Bought and Paid For by Jacqueline Baird
Harlequin Presents® #2291

Penny has no choice but to agree to the
Italian tycoon's offer: he will pay the debts
she owes if she becomes his *wife!* She will be
his wife, bought and paid for—and he wants a
wife in every sense of the word. Penny has
discovered she's still in love with Solo—
but isn't their marriage just a sham…?

Sandra Field

JARED'S LOVE-CHILD

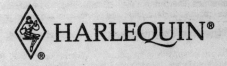

TORONTO • NEW YORK • LONDON
AMSTERDAM • PARIS • SYDNEY • HAMBURG
STOCKHOLM • ATHENS • TOKYO • MILAN • MADRID
PRAGUE • WARSAW • BUDAPEST • AUCKLAND

ISBN 0-373-12288-8

JARED'S LOVE-CHILD

First North American Publication 2002.

Copyright © 1999 by Sandra Field.

This edition published by arrangement with Harlequin Books S.A.

® and TM are trademarks of the publisher. Trademarks indicated with
® are registered in the United States Patent and Trademark Office, the
Canadian Trade Marks Office and in other countries.

Visit us at www.eHarlequin.com

Printed in U.S.A.

CHAPTER ONE

SHE was hot. She was jet-lagged. She was late.

Very late. And the driveway to "The Oaks" was like one of those country roads that go on and on interminably and never arrive anywhere. With a sigh of impatience Devon Fraser wiped the perspiration from her forehead and tried to relax her neck muscles. Just to add to everything else that had gone wrong, she was—and had been for the last fifteen minutes—trapped in a line of limousines and chauffeur-driven Cadillacs occupied by wedding guests who were all early for the wedding. Early and fastidiously attired in formal suits and designer dresses.

Devon was driving her bright red Mazda convertible with the top down and she was wearing the same outfit she'd put on twenty-four hours ago to leave Yemen. A modestly styled and not very becoming green linen suit—now much crumpled—a blouse with a high neck, and undistinguished green pumps that were killing her feet.

No make-up. Almost no sleep. And absolutely no joy at the prospect of the next few hours.

It was her mother's wedding she was late for. Her mother's fifth wedding, to be accurate. This time to a man called Benson Holt. A wealthy man with a son named Jared, of whom Alicia, so she'd said, was terrified. Jared was to be best man to Devon's maid-of-honor.

Devon had spent the last four days in negotiation with some very rich oil barons. She wasn't about to be intimidated by a Toronto playboy called Jared Holt.

The wedding was scheduled for six p.m. and it was now five past five; she'd had to wait for several minutes to pass

through the wrought-iron security gates at the entrance to
Benson Holt's property. It was going to take a small mir-
acle, thought Devon, to get her to "The Oaks" and trans-
form herself in less than an hour from a bedraggled dowd
to a glowing maid-of-honor. All maids-of-honor glowed,
didn't they? Or was that the bride?

Devon didn't know. She'd never been a bride and had
no inclination to change that state of affairs. She could
safely leave being a bride to her mother.

Venerable oak trees lined the driveway, the grass was
velvet-smooth and all the fences—miles of fences—were
painted a pristine white. The prospective groom was indeed
rich. Surprise, surprise, Devon thought sardonically. While
her mother was a professed romantic, Alicia had yet to
marry a poor man.

Through the fences Devon could see open fields and
placid groups of mares and foals, and for a moment she
forgot how unforgivably late she was. She'd remembered
to throw her riding gear into her suitcase in the ten-minute
stop she'd allowed herself at her condo in Toronto. At least
she might get one pleasurable experience out of this wedding. A ride on a thoroughbred.

Because she was, of course, dreading the wedding.

With a jangling of her nerves, she saw that the lane was
widening into a expanse of groomed shrubs and statuary
around a circular driveway. The house was an imposing
mansion of Georgian brick with a great many shutters and
chimneys. Ignoring the directions of the two uniformed
men who were waving the cars to a parking area under the
trees, Devon whipped out of the line-up, skidded to a halt
not twenty feet from the front door and scrambled out,
reaching into the back seat for her case and the long plastic
bag that held her dresses.

Every muscle in her body ached. She felt like hell. And
looked worse.

She ran for the front door. It was flanked by polished coachman's lanterns and was painted a rich dark green. As she reached for the bell, the door swung open.

"Well," a man's voice said mockingly, "the late Miss Fraser."

Devon tucked a stray blond curl into what had been, twenty-four hours ago, a sleek and well-mannered hairdo. "I'm Devon Fraser, yes," she said. "Would you please direct me to my room? I'm in a hurry."

The man was standing in the shadow of the door. Insolently he looked her up and down, from her windblown hair all the way to her dusty and unexciting pumps. "Very late," he added.

Her brief assumption that this was a rather unconventional butler was just that: brief. The man blocking her entrance into the house had never in his life been the servant of others. No, he was the type who gave out the orders, and expected them, unless she was mistaken, to be instantly obeyed.

And then he stepped into the late-afternoon sunlight and for the first time she really saw him. Her eyes widened. Her heart began to hammer in her chest.

A butler? Was she crazy? He was the most magnificent specimen of manhood she'd ever seen.

Tall, dark and handsome didn't begin to describe him.

Certainly he was tall, several inches taller than her five-feet-ten, a fact that instantly irritated her beyond all proportion. His hair was black, his eyes dark as volcanic rock, and for a moment, her imagination working overtime, she saw him as a man who would trail devastation in his wake and bring her only sorrow.

Oh, stop it, Devon! Dozens of men have black hair and dark eyes. Get a grip.

As for handsome, his features were too strong, too infused with sheer male energy, for the word to have much meaning. He was handsome in the same way a polar bear was handsome, she thought. Take one look and run for your life.

Adding to her unease, his expensively tailored tuxedo and crisp white shirt—civilized and sophisticated attire—made him look dangerous rather than civilized, untamed rather than sophisticated. Certainly they did nothing to disguise his breadth of shoulder and depth of chest, his flat belly and lean hips.

He had a beautiful body.

Lots of men had great bodies. But this man exuded male magnetism through his very pores. What woman worthy of the name could resist him?

This one, she thought frantically. Me.

What on earth was going on here? She made it a policy never to be affected by a man's looks or sexual charisma, a policy that had served her well over the years. Kept her from making mistakes like the ones her mother had made. So why was she now slavering over the man in the doorway? Who was, moreover, making her even later for the wedding.

Okay, Devon, calm down, she told herself. You're exhausted and wired all at the same time, you'd rather be in the Kalahari Desert than attending a wedding at "The Oaks," and your imagination's gone on a rampage. A man trailing devastation? Come off it! Sure, his face is much too roughly molded to be called handsome, far too tough and full of determination to be dismissed by any label as facile as playboy. Who cares?

I don't.

But she was certain of one thing. Certain in her bones. The man standing by the glossy green front door was the intimidating Jared Holt. Considerably less inclined to blame her mother for being afraid of him, Devon finally found her voice. "And who might you be?" she asked coolly.

Ignoring her question, he said in a deep baritone as smooth as expensive brandy, "I was hoping you wouldn't turn up at all. So this fiasco of a wedding might at least be postponed."

"Too bad," Devon said. "I'm here." Proud of how normal she sounded, she kept to herself the fact that she too thought of the fast-approaching nuptials as a fiasco. "I presume you're Jared Holt?"

He nodded, making no attempt to shake hands. "You're not at all what I was expecting—your mother keeps raving on about how beautiful you are."

"Dear me," Devon said, "you really don't want my mother and me in the family, do you?"

"You got that right."

"Any more than I want you and your father in mine."

His jaw hardened; it was an extremely determined jaw. "So why didn't you miss your plane from Yemen, Miss Fraser? I don't think your mother would have gone through with the ceremony if you weren't here. You could have scotched the whole thing. At least temporarily."

"Unfortunately," Devon said with icy precision, "I don't see my role in life as my mother's keeper. She may well be intent on making another ill-judged marriage. But she's also over the age of consent. As is your father."

"So you've got claws. How interesting. They don't go with the outfit." And in another of those scathing glances he took in her rumpled linen suit and loose-fitting blouse.

"Mr. Holt, I've spent the last four days negotiating mining rights with some very powerful men who live in a country with different dress codes for women than ours. My plane was late leaving Yemen, I missed my connection in Hamburg, Heathrow was a nightmare of queues and security, and then of all things there was a wildcat strike of baggage handlers in Toronto. Not to mention the traffic getting out of the city. I'm tired and I'm cranky. Why don't you just tell me where my room is so I can get changed?''

''Cranky?'' he repeated with a smile that didn't touch his eyes. ''You should choose your words more carefully—cranky doesn't begin to describe you. You're seething with all kinds of emotions. Typical female, in other words.''

''Generalizations are the sign of a lazy mind,'' Devon said sweetly. ''And the words that would most accurately describe the way I'm feeling aren't the kind of words I'm going to use with a complete stranger. My room, Mr. Holt.''

''So I was right—there's a lot more going on under that meek little exterior of yours than mere cranki-ness...although I fail to understand why you don't want your mother marrying a very rich man. There'll be a lot of spinoffs for you.''

Don't lose it, Devon told herself, gritting her teeth. Jared Holt would like nothing better than for you to scream at him like a harpy five minutes after you arrive on his father's doorstep. She said coldly, ''My mother's been married to men much richer than your father...I have no idea why she's settling for less.'' Delicately she raised one brow. ''Unless, perhaps, he's a great deal more charming than his son?''

''I can be charming when it suits me, and I hate talking to someone who's wearing dark glasses.'' Moving so fast she didn't have time to duck, Jared whipped her glasses off her nose. For a split second she saw the contempt on his face falter, flare into something else altogether. Then that elusive emotion was gone, leaving her to wonder if she'd imagined it.

Whatever it had been, it had again set her heart to racing in her breast.

He said tightly, ''I'll show you to your room. Your

mother's room is next to it. After the wedding, of course, she'll move into my father's wing of the house.''

With an innocent smile Devon said, ''So you have trouble with your father having a sex life, Mr. Holt? Maybe you need a good psychiatrist.''

''I don't care who he sleeps with. I do care who he marries.''

''Control.'' She gave a short laugh. ''Why am I surprised?''

''Let's get something straight right now,'' Jared Holt grated, with such suppressed rage in his voice that Devon had to fight the urge to step backward. ''And you can pass this on to your mother. I will not allow her to take my father to the cleaners when—as is inevitable, given her record—the divorce comes about. Have you got that? Or do I have to repeat it?''

To hell with all her good resolutions. She hadn't traveled thousands of miles to listen to this kind of garbage. ''You know what?'' Devon blazed. ''I've been to forty or fifty different countries in the last eight years and in none of them, not one, have I met a man as gratuitously rude and ignorant as you. You take the cake, Mr. Holt. Congratulations!''

If she'd hoped to get under his skin, she'd failed. His lip curling, he said, ''I'm not being rude—merely honest. Not a trait you recognize, Devon Fraser? But perhaps you're just not used to it.''

For Devon the game, if that was what it was, had suddenly gone on too long. She said sharply, ''Are you figuring on trading cheap shots with me until it's time for the wedding? Hoping my mother will call it off at the last minute if she thinks I'm not here? I'm sorry to disappoint you, but I'm perfectly capable of finding her on my own, thank you very much.'' And she took two steps past him.

Again he moved so swiftly she scarcely even saw the

movement. His hand closed around her sleeve; its grip was as tight and impersonal as a circle of steel. Devon wasn't used to having to crane her neck to look up into a man's face; she was too tall for that and wasn't above using her height when it suited her. But Jared Holt made her feel diminished and ridiculously unsure of herself. Not certain which she hated more, that sensation or the man himself, she rapped, "Let go of me!"

"Calm down," he said sardonically, "I was only going to show you to your room." He reached round her, the scent of his aftershave drifting to her nostrils, his dark head so close she could have stroked his hair, and took her suitcase from her unresisting fingers. "Although," he went on, "time's running out, and I've never yet known a woman who could get ready for anything in less than an hour."

She wanted to run her fingers through his hair, find out if it was as silky as it looked. No use denying it. Oh God, what was wrong with her?

With a hollow sinking in her belly, Devon strove for control, praying her crazy impulse hadn't shown in her face. Coating her features with disdain, she looked him up and down. "I'm sure you've known a lot of women."

"You could say so."

"In my opinion, the man who has to boast of his conquests isn't worth bothering about."

"Those with little experience of men, Miss Fraser, have to make do with opinions."

Obviously he thought her too unattractive to get herself a man. Gritting her teeth, Devon said, "Some of us prefer to choose our experiences! You look good, I'll give you that. But a man—again in my opinion—should be a touch more substantial than the packaging."

"You have a lot of opinions about men for a woman whose packaging doesn't warrant a second look!"

You'll pay for that, Devon seethed inwardly. I'll make

you give me more than a second look, you arrogant playboy! The plastic carrier over her arm contained two dresses, one entirely correct for a high society wedding, the other rather more interesting but by no means as correct. She now knew which one she was going to wear. Decision made.

Although if she were smart she'd go for the dull but safe dress. Because by far the worst thing about this absurd conversation was the fact that she found Jared so extraordinarily attractive. Male to her female at the most basic of levels. He exuded a sexual confidence that irritated her intensely, partly because she was sure it was completely unconscious. He wasn't trying to attract her. Oh, no. She wasn't worth the time or the effort.

But the ease of his stance, the shiny lock of dark hair falling so casually over his tanned forehead, the latent strength of his fingers—every molecule of his body— tugged her toward him even as every word he'd said warned her to run as far and as fast as she could. She'd managed very nicely the last few years by keeping her own sexuality under wraps. If Jared Holt attracted and infuriated her, he also frightened her. Deeply.

"You're very quiet," he taunted. "Don't tell me you've run out of opinions already?"

"They're wasted on you."

He said with savage emphasis, "This whole day is wasted on me."

"Then—at last—we agree on something."

With sudden impatience he pulled her through the door, kicked it shut behind him and marched her across a generous and sun-filled hallway toward the graceful curve of a mahogany stairwell. More than his fingers were strong, Devon thought with a shiver of her nerves. Although she kept herself in very good physical condition, she knew it would be useless to resist him; he could overpower her without even exerting himself. Resting her hand on the banister, her one desire to puncture his intolerable ego, she said with assumed lightness, "I did compliment you, you know."

"I must have missed it," Jared said tersely.

"Your good looks, remember? The packaging. You look rather familiar to me...although I can't place you. Have you ever done any modeling?"

"I have not!"

She'd gotten to him. Hurray, hurray. Taking her time going up the stairs, gazing at all the portraits of the race-horses for which Benson Holt was famous, Devon said pleasantly, "What beautiful creatures...perhaps you work for your father in the stables, Mr. Holt?"

He bit off the words. "No. I don't."

Score two. "Then what do you do?"

"Try and keep fortune hunters away from him. At which I've obviously screwed up." He led her into a separate wing and pushed open a white-panelled door. "Your mother's in the end room, this one's yours. They both have private bathrooms."

Before Devon could protest he'd walked in and was putting her case down by the bed. She didn't want him in here. She didn't want him anywhere near her or a bed or any combination of the two. She said amiably, "Do try and smile for the cameras, won't you? Unless you want all the wedding albums to show you sulking like a little boy who didn't get his own way."

"Don't tell me what to do," Jared said softly. "I don't like it."

Her breath caught in her throat and her heart gave an uneasy lurch. From the very first she'd thought him dangerous. And she'd been right. But something in her refused to back down, no matter how intimidating he was. Devon said, "How interesting...I also hate being ordered around. Something else we have in common."

"Unfortunately we're going to have far too much in common. I can't imagine you'll like being my stepsister any more than I'll enjoy being your stepbrother. Thanksgiving and Christmas in the same house. Family birthdays. On and on it goes." He gave her a wolfish grin. "You and I will be tied together once this marriage takes place—one more reason you should have missed your plane."

She said steadily, "My job—I'm a lawyer who negotiates mining rights—requires I spend a large part of the year out of the country. You might be available for every family birthday that comes along. I won't be."

Jared reached over and tucked a strand of hair behind her ear; as his hand streaked her neck with fire, it took every ounce of Devon's control to keep her face immobile. He said smoothly, "Talking of wedding photos, I hope you're planning on doing something with your hair in the next forty minutes. But don't keep us waiting, will you, Miss Fraser? That's the bride's prerogative."

He strode across the carpet and shut the door very quietly behind him. Devon dropped the plastic carrier on her bed and took half a dozen long, steadying breaths. The room seemed bigger without him. Bigger and emptier. Then a tap came at the door and she jumped as though a gun had gone off in her ear. "Yes?" she quavered.

"Darling, is that you?"

"Come in, Mother," Devon said, and braced herself.

"Jared told me you'd arrived. I've been so worried, I thought you weren't going to make it in time, and I really need your support—Jared looks at me as though I'm the original scarlet woman, quite frankly he terrifies me. I can't imagine how Benson fathered him...darling, you're not even dressed!"

"That's because I've only just arrived," Devon said, and

kissed her mother's exquisitely made-up cheek and looked her up and down. "You look lovely," she said truthfully.

"I didn't want to wear white—not really suitable. Do I really look all right?" And anxiously Alicia tweaked at the long skirt of her cream-colored silk dress.

For once Alicia had avoided the frills, lace and beadwork that were her normal adornment. The dress was elegant, and her hairdo equally restrained. It was five months since Devon had seen her, at which time Benson Holt had simply been a name Alicia had dropped into the conversation rather more often than was necessary. For the first time wondering if Benson had brought about other changes, Devon said, "It's a wonderful dress! Show me your ring."

With a shyness that Devon scarcely thought appropriate, considering this was her mother's fifth engagement ring, Alicia held out her left hand. The diamond blazed in its ornate setting. Devon had never been fond of diamonds; their cold glitter never looked anything other than mercenary to her. "I hope you'll be very happy," she said.

Alicia gave a hunted look at her gold watch. "The ceremony begins in thirty-five minutes."

"Then you'd better get out of here and let me get ready," Devon said, smiling. "I'm sorry I'm so late. You know I'd originally planned to be here for last night's rehearsal dinner—but between Yemen and here it was one delay after another."

"I had to sit between Benson and Jared." Alicia gave a shudder of pure nerves. "Do you know what he did three days ago? Jared, I mean. He tried to buy me off."

"He *what*?"

"He offered me a great deal of money to call off the wedding. And I can't even tell Benson; Jared is his only son, after all."

"How *dare* he do that?"

"He'd dare anything. He's the head of Holt

Incorporated. Millions of dollars, darling. Millions. He didn't make those by pussyfooting around."

Devon's jaw dropped. "Jared Holt runs Holt Incorporated?"

"He doesn't just run it. He owns it. He's made a fortune; he's fifty times richer than Benson."

Holt Incorporated involved chains of resorts the world over, some of which Devon had stayed in, a fleet of cruise ships, several commodity conglomerates and an outstandingly successful computer company. "Why didn't you tell me?" Devon croaked.

With some of her normal spirit Alicia said, "Long distance? From Borneo and Papua New Guinea and all those other places you're always going to? I've got better things to talk about than Jared Holt."

Devon sat down on the bed and said with a gurgle of laughter, "Guess what? I asked him if he worked in his father's stables."

"Darling, you didn't!"

"And before that I wanted to know if he'd ever done any modeling."

Alicia groaned. "Oh, no...how *could* you?"

"Very easily. He's the rudest and most arrogant man I've ever met in my entire life. And I've met a few."

Alicia gave a little shiver. "You don't want to cross him. He'd make a bad enemy, Devon."

Her mother only called her Devon when she meant business. "I'm not scared of Jared Holt," Devon said, not altogether accurately. "But I am scared of arriving half an hour late at that charming arbour I saw set up in the garden. Out, Mother. I've got to get ready."

Alicia gave her a quick, fervent hug. "I'm so glad you're here," she said, and clicked the door shut behind her.

Wishing she could feel the same way, Devon unzipped her case, shook out one of the two dresses, and headed for the shower.

CHAPTER TWO

AT ONE minute to six Alicia tapped on Devon's door. "Are you ready, darling?"

Devon was standing in front of the full-length mirror outlining her mouth in Luscious Pink. "Come in, Mother. Two seconds more," she called, and swiftly filled in the outline. Then she inserted long drop earrings made of Australian opals, deeply blue and iridescent.

"I'm a nervous wreck," Alicia babbled. "I know this is my fifth wedding, but I truly love Benson and I really want this one to last forever. For all of us to be one happy family. Do you think I should marry him, Devon, or do you think I'm making another terrible mistake?"

As Devon had yet to meet Benson, she could scarcely answer this question. Although if Benson was anything like Jared, her mother was making the biggest mistake of her marital career. And "one happy family" was sure to be a pipe dream. Christmas with Jared Holt? Devon would rather die. "Of course you'll be happy," she said soothingly, seeing with a twinge of compassion that her mother's lips were quivering. Briefly she tucked Alicia's arm in hers and said, gazing at their joint reflections in the mirror, "Come on, Ma, let's go knock 'em out."

"The flowers are on the table in the hall...we do look rather nice, don't we?" Alicia said naively.

"Nice" wasn't the effect Devon had been aiming for. Her dress, a long shimmer of turquoise Thai silk, was artfully simple, its neckline cut so that it cupped her breasts, its slim-fitting skirt slit to the knee. Another opal nestled in her cleavage; her shoes were thin-strapped sandals with

18

very high heels. She'd piled her hair on her head, a few curls casually caressing her neck and her cheeks. "We're gorgeous," Devon said. "And don't you dare let Jared Holt ruin your wedding day; he's not worth it."

"I won't," Alicia said, and gave her daughter a militant smile. "I'm learning a few things, Devon. I told Benson I wouldn't promise to obey, I was too old for that. He just laughed and said he didn't want a doormat for a wife. He's a very nice man; you'll like him."

The romantic Italian, the British aristocrat and the Texas oilman, husbands two, three and four, had all been introduced to Devon in a similar manner; Alicia always wanted her daughter to like the prospective groom. Devon said diplomatically, "I'm looking forward to meeting him."

The flowers were clusters of pale orchids and the photographer was waiting for them. Feeling her heart begin to beat uncomfortably fast, Devon picked up the smaller of the two bouquets and smiled obediently into the camera. Then she walked down the stairs at her mother's side. As they reached the bottom step, Alicia said, "I did ask you to give me away, darling, didn't I?"

Devon almost tripped over the faded Ushak runner on the hall floor. "Nope."

"Benson's brother-in-law was to have done it. But he had an operation for varicose veins two weeks ago. The only other choice was Jared. Please say you'll do it, Devon!"

Allow that cynical, overbearing creep to escort her mother up the aisle? No way. "Sure I will," said Devon.

After they'd emerged into the sunshine on the front step, the photographer took several shots of them gazing in a heartfelt manner into their bouquets. Devon in the meantime was sneaking peaks at the set-up. White awnings stretched between the trees, providing shade from the sun. Baskets of mock-orange, roses and delphiniums flanked the array of wicker chairs where the guests were seated, and the soft ripple of harp music fell over their chatter.

Finally the photographer was satisfied. As Alicia and Devon approached the chairs, the harpist drew one last chord from her instrument and fell silent. From an organ near the white flower-bedecked altar came the first notes of the wedding processional. It was being played, Devon noticed abstractedly, with very little regard for either rhythm or accuracy.

Alicia whispered, "That's Benson's sister at the organ. She insisted. Benson didn't want to hurt her feelings. Oh, Devon, I'm so nervous. I should never have agreed to marry him. Why do I keep getting married? I'm not young, like you; I should know better."

"Come on, Mother, it's too late now. So let's do it in style," Devon said, took her mother's hand and drew it through her arm, and then struggled to establish some kind of accord between their steps and the music. It wasn't easy. But it did take her mind off the array of guests, the waiting clergyman, and the two men standing in front of the altar. Benson, the groom, and Jared, his son. Both had their backs to the two women pacing up the green carpet that had been laid over the grass.

Benson was shorter than his son and had a well-groomed crop of gray hair. As the organ hit a sharp instead of a flat, he turned, saw Alicia walking toward him and smiled at her. He wasn't as handsome as Jared and his waist had a comfortable thickness. He looked human, thought Devon. Unlike Jared. And his smile was both loving and kind. Also unlike Jared.

Kindness was right up there on Devon's list of virtues. She had long ago decided you couldn't fake it.

Well, she thought, how interesting. And not at all what I was expecting. She whispered into her mother's ear, "I think you picked a good 'un, Mother,'' and was rewarded with a watery and grateful smile from Alicia.

The organ emitted an uncertain twiddle, then managed to land on a chord that was loud, triumphant and startlingly off-key. Devon shuddered. And finally Jared turned his head.

He didn't even look at Alicia. His gaze went straight to Alicia's daughter, and for a most satisfactory moment that she knew she wasn't imagining Devon saw blank shock rigidify every muscle of his face. She lowered her lids demurely, as befitted a woman with very little experience. A woman whose packaging, to quote him, didn't warrant a second look. Then she allowed the most innocent of smiles to play on her lips.

But when she looked up, her smile was directed solely at Benson.

Right up until the last minute, Jared had thought he'd have to give Alicia away: a duty he would have performed punctiliously and with genuine loathing. But as he and Benson had left the house via the conservatory, his father had said, "Alicia's going to ask Devon to give her away. So you're off the hook."

Annoyed with himself for having made his distaste for the task so obvious, Jared said shortly, "I met her. The daughter, I mean. She's not what I'd expected. She's tall and frumpy with a tongue like a chainsaw."

"Really? Alicia showed me a photo—I thought she was very pretty."

"A good photographer can make a rose out of a cactus."

Benson said abruptly, "Have you got the ring?"

"Yes, Dad—you've asked me that twice already."

"There's Martin, waving at us. Time to take our places."

Martin was the butler; his signal meant that Alicia was

ready. Jared glanced at his watch. Seven minutes past six. Devon Fraser was remarkably prompt. For a woman.

He followed his father under the shade of the awning, nodded at the clergyman and studiously avoided looking at the guests. Lise was presumably somewhere in that crush. She'd cajoled him for an invitation, and he'd made the mistake of sending her one. He was going to have to decide what to do about Lise, he thought, and winced as Aunt Bessie attacked the portable organ with her usual gusto and total disregard for the printed score. If he, Jared, were ever foolish enough to get married—a stupid proposition; he had no intention of allowing himself to be tied for life to one woman—he'd get married on his yacht. Aunt Bessie suffered from seasickness. Aunt Bessie wouldn't set foot on anything remotely resembling the deck of a ship.

From the corner of his eye he saw his father turn and smile at his prospective bride. He was about to become her fifth husband. Anger coiled tight in Jared's gut. He'd done his best to talk his father out of this ill-advised wedding, and then he'd tried a little judicious bribery of Alicia. Neither of which had worked. Even though he'd offered Alicia a very considerable sum.

She could get more from a divorce settlement; that, he was sure, had been her reasoning.

He was damned if he was going to smile at Alicia. At least the clergyman had insisted the photographer keep his distance during the ceremony. So if he, Jared, didn't feel like smiling at anyone, he didn't have to.

Devon Fraser had claimed he was sulking because he hadn't gotten his own way. Had he ever known a woman to get so quickly and so thoroughly under his skin?

Another of Aunt Bessie's chords screeched along his nerves. Surely Alicia and her daughter were nearly at the altar—they could have walked from Central Park to the

Bronx by now. Fighting down his impatience, Jared looked around to check on their progress.

A tall woman in a shimmer of turquoise was walking toward him, looking straight at him, her head held high.

Her beauty slammed into his chest as though he'd been punched, hard, on the breastbone.

Her hair was heaped on her head, and shone like ripe wheat, baring the slim line of her throat. Her shoulders rose from her dress in impossibly elegant curves; the swell of her breasts made his heart thud as though he'd dropped a twenty- kilo weight. Ripe breasts. Full breasts. Voluptuous breasts, their pale sheen like the petals of the orchids she was carrying. In her cleavage a blue stone shot sparks of fire.

Her hips swayed gracefully as she walked; under the gleaming silk skirt her legs seemed to go on forever.

But it was her eyes that held him. Those exquisitely wide-spaced eyes that had so disconcerted him when he'd pulled off her sunglasses on the front step. He'd been expecting mousy brown, or light gray. Anything but irises the brilliant blue of a tropical sea. Eyes he could drown in.

As his groin tightened involuntarily, Jared knew with every fiber of his being that he wouldn't rest until he had Devon Fraser in his bed. Until he possessed her in the most primitive of ways.

This was the woman whose packaging he'd derided? The woman he'd labelled a frump? Was he losing his marbles?

With a faraway part of his brain, the only part that still seemed to be functioning, Jared suddenly realized that Devon was fully aware of the effect she was having on him, and that his response had pleased her enormously. Then she dropped her lids, the smallest of smiles playing on the soft pink curves of her mouth.

A kissable mouth. A deliciously seductive mouth.

Damn you, Devon Fraser, Jared thought vengefully. You

took me in with your high-necked blouse and your rumpled suit and your washed-out cheeks. Took me in but good. But you won't do it again. Not twice in one day.

Because I'm going to teach you a lesson. I don't know how yet. But I'll figure out something.

I don't like being jerked around by a woman. Made to look like a fool. I don't like that at all. Before this farce of a wedding's over, you're going to wish you hadn't done it.

With a small jolt he realized the clergyman was clearing his throat, and that the four of them were now neatly lined up in front of all the guests. Pay attention, Jared. Forget Devon Fraser, at least for the next few minutes. You're supposed to be the best man.

May the best man win.

He didn't know where that line had come from. But he did know he meant it as far as Devon was concerned. She might have won the first round. She wasn't going to win the second. He was going to get his revenge one way or another.

Revenge was a strong word.

The sonorous, old-fashioned words of the marriage service rolled over him. Devon's profile was turned to him: a straight nose and decided chin, the gleaming weight of her hair. He wanted to pull out the pins and let it tumble to her shoulders. He wanted to thread his fingers in its soft sheen, and through it caress the rise of her breasts. He wanted to push her flat on satin sheets and lower his body onto hers until... He was doing it again, he thought viciously. What the hell was wrong with him? She was a woman, that was all. One more woman.

She'd be willing. Of course. They all were.

Which was the crux of the problem.

He was an extremely rich man. He wielded a lot of power in the places where it mattered. Plus there was something about his looks and his body—he knew this without vanity—that women found attractive. Add to that the fact that he was unmarried and what did you have? A challenge that every female between the ages of eighteen and forty-five thought they should take up.

It would be a change, he thought cynically, to be seen for once as a man. Just a man. Instead of a corporate figurehead wrapped in thousand dollar bills.

Some chance. Women didn't operate that way.

Trouble was, he was also bored to the back teeth with all the games. He knew every move from beginning to end. The first date, the artful questions, the intimate dinner—during which he always made his boundaries plain: the relationship had to be on his terms or not at all. But very few of them listened, and if they did they took it as another challenge—to achieve what other women hadn't been able to. Then there was the first kiss, the gifts he got his secretary to send, the flowers. The lovemaking, the pouting when he made it plain that, no, he wouldn't stay overnight; he never did. The inevitable expectations of commitment. The anger or the weeping—depending on the woman—when for the second time he made it clear that he didn't share those expectations, he wasn't into commitment. Never had been, never would be. Then, last of all, the break-up.

The last few years he'd played the game less and less. Lise was an example of his breaking of the pattern. He was honest enough with himself to know he was using Lise as protective coloration: if his social circle assumed he was having an affair with her, it kept the majority of the other women at bay, as well as the gossip columnists. Very few of his compatriots would have believed he wasn't sleeping with Lise. She sure wasn't going to tell them; he knew that much. She was using him just as blatantly as he was using her. To be seen as the mistress of Jared Holt was a boost for Lise's ego—and for her career.

As for his sexual needs, he'd been subduing those for months in a ferocious focus on his far-flung business empire, and by engaging in strenuous athletic pursuits in various untamed parts of the world.

In the last few minutes Devon Fraser had put paid to all that. Since his first glimpse of her in that dress his sexuality had been running rampant. He knew what he wanted. And he wanted it soon.

Her dress, he thought caustically, had cost money. Big bucks. That stunning combination of elegance and provocation didn't come cheap. So was she also after him, one more woman chasing after the security of a big bankroll? Like mother, like daughter?

Except the daughter was twenty years younger and ten times more beautiful.

Alicia had snagged Benson with very little effort. So now was it Devon's turn to get the head of the company, the one with the real bucks? She was just being a little more subtle about it than all the other females of his acquaintance.

Subtle? Or downright devious? Keep on track, Jared, he told himself. After all, Devon could scarcely be said to have encouraged him on the front steps of his father's house. Neither in her dress or her conversation.

Could he be mistaken? Was she genuinely as antagonistic toward him as she'd seemed?

"Who gives this woman to be married to this man?"

Devon said clearly, "I do," gave her mother a smile that made Jared's heart lurch in his chest, and stepped a little to one side. He fought to pay attention to the service: he'd really look an idiot if he flubbed his own cue.

He'd already made an idiot of himself once in front of Devon Fraser. He was damned if he was going to do it twice in one day.

*   *   *

Devon had been to lots of weddings, for by now most of her contemporaries were married. She'd thought she was immune to the whole ritual. Yet today for some reason the words, so simple yet so powerful, had gone straight through her. "To love and to cherish..." Who, except for her almost forgotten father, had ever cherished her? Not Alicia, she'd been too busy chasing romance from one continent to the next. Not any of her stepfathers. Certainly not Steve, who'd been her lover for over three years. Or, more recently, Peter. Who, luckily, hadn't become her lover.

So what? She didn't need cherishing; she was an independent, intelligent, thirty-two-year-old woman who excelled at a difficult job and who'd constructed her whole life so as to avoid intimacy and long-term relationships.

Then why was she feeling as weepy as any bride?

"...till death do us part."

Alicia had been parted from Devon's father by death. Devon's father, according to Alicia, had been the love of her life—a story clung to more obsessively with every ensuing divorce. Devon had been seven when he died. She could remember as clearly as if it were yesterday that she'd been out in the garden when her mother had told her. The blackberries had been ripe and a thrush had been singing in the walnut tree...

Oh God, she felt far weepier than any bride. She wouldn't cry; she wouldn't! Apart from anything else it would only confirm Jared Holt's low estimation of women. Emotional basket cases, that was how he saw the female sex. Irrational, completely at the mercy of their feelings. Not like him.

Jared had passed his father the ring and the clergyman was intoning the age-old symbolic words. Nervously Devon eased Benson's ring from her thumb. Suddenly it slipped through her fingers and fell into the midst of the orchids. She scrabbled for it, bruising the sleek, expensive petals;

when it didn't emerge, she gave the bouquet a shake, and with an inward moan of dismay watched the ring plummet to the ground and roll along the green carpet. Toward Jared.

He moved very swiftly for so big a man. Stooping, he grabbed the ring and passed it to her. His eyes were looking straight into hers. They weren't black, as she'd thought when she'd been standing on the front step. They were a dark midnight blue, impenetrable and cold as a winter sky. Her lashes flickered. Gingerly, trying not to touch him, she plucked the ring from his open palm, hearing the low murmur of amusement from the congregation. Blushing scarlet, she passed the ring to her mother.

Let this be over soon, please, she prayed. Let me get out of here without disgracing myself. Without revealing to anyone—especially Jared—how fragile I feel.

He probably already knows. He doesn't miss a trick, that man.

Benson kissed his new wife with decorum. Her mother, Devon noticed distantly, looked flushed and very happy. Then Aunt Bessie swung into action again, pulling out all the stops. Benson took Alicia's hand in his with a big grin, and started down the aisle between the ranked chairs. Now it's our turn, Devon thought. Mine and Jared's.

She turned to him with a brilliant smile, resting her fingers on the arm he was proffering, not at all surprised to feel the muscles taut as stretched cable.

With a deliberation that was somehow terrifying, he put his own hand on top of hers. The heat of his skin burned into her flesh like a brand; the raw hunger in his eyes filled her with panic. Then, suddenly, the hunger was gone, vanished as if it had never been.

Turned off, as though by a switch.

Every nerve in her body screamed at her to beware. She dragged her gaze away from his and smiled into the sea of faces, dimly rather proud of her composure. With a superhuman effort she retrieved her voice, saying lightly, "Your aunt is excelling herself."

"You got a real kick out of shoving that dress in my face, didn't you?"

He towered over her, even when she was wearing high heels. Devon looked up at him limpidly and said in a voice as smooth as cream, "At this precise moment we're being observed by a couple of hundred socialites, some of whom I assume are friends of yours...do try and control your temper. As for your aunt, any musician worth her salt should be able to improvise."

"She never does anything but improvise, and I really hate being made a fool of."

The photographer planted himself in front of them and angled the camera at their faces. "Just a little closer to her, Mr. Holt. Big smile—that's great."

Blinded by the flash, horribly aware of the jut of Jared's hip and the hard line of his shoulder, Devon stumbled on a fold of the carpet. Quickly Jared's arm went round her waist, and for a moment all her weight was resting on him. Instinctively she knew that with very little effort he could have picked her up and carried her the rest of the way. One arm around her hips, the other pressing her to his chest...

Was she losing her mind?

She pushed free of him, struggling for composure, and with huge relief saw that Benson and Alicia were waiting for them. "Mother, congratulations," Devon said warmly, kissing Alicia on the cheek. Then she held out her hand to Benson. "I'm so happy to meet you," she said. "I'm only sorry I had to wait until you were all the way to the altar."

Benson planted a kiss on her cheek. "Devon...a pleasure. You're almost as beautiful as your mother."

Alicia gave a delighted giggle, and Devon heard Jared's breath hiss between his teeth. "You're much better-looking than your son," she responded cordially. "I wish you both every happiness."

As Alicia hugged her again, spilling out how nervous she'd been and how relieved she was that the ceremony was over, Benson drew his son aside. "You need glasses, boy," he said in a jovial undertone. "A frump? The girl's gorgeous!"

"You should have seen her," Jared muttered. "It looked like she'd slept in her suit for a week and her hair was—"

"Bifocals," Benson interrupted, clapping Jared on the arm.

Jared bit his tongue. Bad enough that Devon had made a fool of him; he didn't need his father rubbing it in. But he'd get even, he thought, if it took him the rest of the day. Devon had used her sexuality—not to mention that blue dress—to get at him; he just might use his own sexuality in revenge. God knows enough women had made it clear how attractive he was.

He would show Devon Fraser she shouldn't play with fire. And what enormous pleasure that would give him.

"You're very quiet, Jared," Alicia said provocatively.

Jared gave himself a mental shake, pasted a smile on his face, and with impeccable good manners congratulated his new stepmother and his father on their marriage. An ordinary observer couldn't have faulted him. But Devon, attuned to him in a way that disconcerted her, could see the stiffness in his shoulders and hear the reservations in his voice. He was playing to the audience. And he didn't mean a word of it.

The four of them then formed an impromptu receiving line. The faces passed in front of Devon in a blur, Jared's manners irreproachable as he said, time after time, "May I introduce Alicia's daughter to you?...Miss Devon Fraser."

Aunt Bessie stood out from the crowd. Aunt Bessie was

wearing orange shantung and a lime-green hat; her fingers were so cluttered with diamonds Devon was amazed she'd been able to play any notes at all, right or wrong. She kissed her nephew and said in a piercing voice, "Time you got yourself hitched, Jared. You're not getting any younger."

"You married Uncle Leonard instead of waiting for me," Jared said. "It broke my heart."

Aunt Bessie chuckled, looking from him to Devon. "Now this young lady looks like she'd be your match," she remarked. "You must be Alicia's daughter."

"I'm Devon, yes."

"Don't let him fool you with that big-businessman act. Heart of gold." She gave another raucous chuckle. "Pockets full of gold, too. You after his money?"

Devon said crisply, "I'm not after him at all. Despite your recommendation."

"That's what you need, Jared, a woman who'll stick up for herself." Jared's aunt leaned toward Devon. "Too many of 'em let him walk all over them. Not good for him."

"Aunt Bessie," Jared said, "you're holding up the line."

"I'll talk to you later, dear," Aunt Bessie said, squeezing Devon's fingers meaningfully. Then, with some determination, she waddled off toward the nearest tray of champagne.

Not if I can help it, thought Devon, and smiled at the next guest, whose name totally escaped her. She had the beginnings of a headache and a whole bottle of champagne was starting to seem like a very viable option.

Then a female voice said warmly, "Darling—I'm so sorry I missed you before the wedding."

Devon blinked as the owner of the voice pulled Jared's head down and kissed him explicitly on the lips.

Ownership, Devon thought intuitively. A public display of ownership, that's what this kiss is all about.

So why wasn't she feeling relieved that Jared Holt was already spoken for?

CHAPTER THREE

THE woman kissing Jared was dainty, the kind of female who always made Devon feel outsized. She was also extremely chic, with a porcelain complexion and a cap of gleaming black hair; her pale pink raw silk suit screamed Paris.

Jared wasn't exactly fighting her off. When he did raise his head, he had frosted pink lipstick on his mouth. A mouth, Devon thought unwillingly, that was both strongly and sensually carved. A very masculine mouth.

He said unhurriedly, "Hello, Lise...I was with Dad before the wedding, figured he needed the moral support. May I introduce the bride's daughter, Devon Fraser? Devon, this is my friend Lise Lamont, from Manhattan. Lise is a Broadway actress."

Lise had pale blue eyes, her least attractive feature. They didn't look enthralled at meeting Devon. Devon said politely, "How do you do, Miss Lamont? I believe I saw you in the last Stan Niall play...a challenging role that you more than fulfilled."

Lise inclined her head regally. "Thank you. Jared was a great support to me during that run." She gave a delicate shudder. "I thought it would never end—you were so good to me, darling."

So Jared and Lise went back a while. And Devon happened to know that Holt Incorporated had its headquarters in New York. Unquestionably Lise was staking her claim to Jared. Hands off, Devon. That was the message.

Two could play that game, thought Devon, and said casually, "I'm glad I managed to squeeze in a visit to the theater for your play—I was between trips to Argentina and South Africa." I have, in other words, more important things to do with my life than keep my hands on or off Jared Holt.

Lise's smile never faltered. "You must try and attend Marguerite Hammlin's new play. I was fortunate enough to get the lead—an extraordinarily powerful part." She let her fingers linger on Jared's sleeve. "I'll see you after the dinner, darling."

In a wave of expensive perfume she drifted away. Two more army colonels and a couple of horse breeders followed, and then at the very end of the line a lanky, bespectacled young man with intelligent gray eyes, who was wearing a suit that badly needed pressing. "Hi, Jared, good to see you. It was snowing in Nanasivik this morning so the Twin Otter was late…I only just arrived." He smiled at Devon. "You must be Alicia's daughter…you're very like your mother."

Jared said stiffly, "Devon, this is Patrick Kendall, my cousin. Aunt Bessie's son."

Devon warmed to him instantly. "What were you doing on Baffin Island, Patrick?"

"I'm a geologist—I was taking core samples in the area."

"I was there just a month ago," Devon said, explaining some of the ramifications of her job.

Patrick's questions were as intelligent as his eyes, and it was Jared who interrupted them. "Aunt Bessie's waving at you, Patrick—shouldn't you say hello to her?"

"Guess I'd better…I'll catch you after dinner, Devon."

The receiving line was done. Devon's feet were killing her. She rested her weight on one foot and wriggled her sore toes. "I like your cousin," she said, glancing up at Jared. "By the way, your actress friend left lipstick on you."

"Patrick's okay. Although he'll never be anything but a two-bit geologist."

"He strikes me as a happy man," Devon said coldly.

"Hasn't got two cents to rub together."

"Let's get something straight, Jared," she announced. "It's very obvious to me that you're obsessed with money. I am not, repeat not, after even a single dollar that belongs to you. I prefer to earn my own money."

Jared fished a white handkerchief from his pocket. "Wipe the lipstick off, would you?"

He didn't believe her. Although briefly Devon thought of refusing his request, there was a glint in his eye that told her he'd think her a coward were she to refuse. She took the smooth white linen and rubbed Aunt Bessie's smear of tangerine from his cheek and then Lise's more refined pale pink from his mouth, all the while keeping thought and feeling under rigid control. Jared stood very still, watching her. When she'd finished, he said, "There's none of your lipstick on me."

"Nor will there be."

"Seems a pity." He took the handkerchief from her, captured her fingers in his and raised them to his lips, kissing them slowly, one by one.

Devon's heart seemed to stop beating. The heat of his mouth burned through all her defences; his downbent head made him seem momentarily vulnerable. She didn't think she'd ever been the recipient of so seductive or unexpected a gesture.

Like an ambush, desire snaked through her, fierce and compelling. Her body swayed toward him, her ill-fated bouquet dropping to the floor so that she could rest her hand on his black hair, finding it, as she had expected, thick and silky to the touch. As an ache of primal need blossomed deep inside her, her surroundings fell away, leaving only her and Jared in the world. Seducer and seduced.

He straightened, let go of her hand and said coolly, "So you're as willing as the rest of them...I don't know why I should be surprised."

It was as if he'd slapped her in the face. Feeling the crimson of humiliation creep up her cheeks, Devon said tautly, "It's all a game to you, isn't it?"

A game called revenge, he thought grimly. "Just like that dress was a game."

And how could she deny it? She'd worn the dress out of pique and a desire to shock him. "So now we're even," she said. "I got you. You got me. But I don't want to play any more, Jared. Game over."

"According to you."

"You're already taken. Lise made that clear."

"I don't belong to any woman," Jared said with dangerous emphasis.

"Tell that to Lise. Not to me. I'm not interested."

"You could have fooled me."

"Jared, half the guests are staring at us and the other half are trying to hear what we're saying. And I badly need— in short order—at least three glasses of champagne."

"In that case, we'll have to continue this later."

"There's nothing to continue!"

But Jared was signaling to the nearest white-coated waiter. He took two glasses from the silver tray and passed her one. "Welcome to the family, Devon."

The champagne was as ice-cold as ocean foam. After a swift glance around, Devon raised her glass and said gently, "Go to hell, Jared."

He gave a choke of laughter. "I'll say one thing for you. Your tactics are different than most."

"You're in a bad way when you confuse truth with tactics."

"Truth and the weaker sex don't belong in the same category."

"Truth and integrity do!"

"A woman's integrity, my darling Devon, is married to a man's bank account."

It was Devon's turn to laugh. "All women are gold-diggers? What a cliché! Surely the head of Holt Incorporated can do better than that."

"If you knew I was the head of Holt Incorporated," he rasped, "why did you ask if I worked in the stables?"

"For the obvious reason that at that time I didn't know."

"When did you find out?"

"My mother told me right after you left my room."

"Whereupon you put on that amazingly provocative dress. I rest my case."

Devon snapped, "I put on this dress because I thought you were the rudest man I'd ever met and I wanted to take you down a peg or two. Some chance. Your ego's impenetrable."

"Perhaps Aunt Bessie was right—I've met my match."

Devon took a big gulp of champagne, sneezed twice as the bubbles went up her nose, and said haughtily, "My ego's a grain of sand compared to yours—yours is as big as a boulder. Now will you please excuse me? I have better things to do at this wedding than trade insults with you."

Unfortunately she then planted her foot squarely on her bouquet. Glaring at him, daring him to laugh at her, she said, "You were right about one thing, Jared Holt—I should have missed the plane in Yemen."

She stooped, revealing rather a lot of leg in the process, grabbed the battered orchids and stalked off in the general direction of her mother. And with every nerve in her body Devon was aware that Jared was watching her.

She made rather febrile conversation with a lot of people, then to her relief saw that the master of ceremonies was ushering them toward a peaked tent decorated with banners and mounds of garden flowers, where dinner was to be

served. A chamber orchestra was playing some bouncy
Mozart. Devon, of course, was at the head table. To her
dismay, she saw she was seated between Benson and his
son. Aunt Bessie's husband, he of the varicose veins, was
on her mother's other side.

It was too late to switch the name cards. She gave
Benson an insincere smile as he pulled out her chair, and
sat down. A gilt-edged plate of piping hot scallops in puff
pastry was put in front of her. She stared at the scallops,
wishing she hadn't drunk so much champagne, wondering
how long it was since she last ate a proper meal. Too long.
The pastry wavered in her vision.

Hastily she bent down to shove her ruined bouquet under
the table, feeling the blood rush back to her head. She
didn't care if she ever saw another orchid in her entire life.
Or scallop.

Hard fingers encircled her elbow, drawing her back up-
right. Jared said tightly, "Are you all right?"

She gaped at him, mumbling, "I'm fine…I—I just can't
remember when—or where—I last ate a real meal. Yemen,
I suppose. Was it yesterday?"

Jared grabbed a roll from a nearby basket, split it and
passed her a piece. "Here, eat this."

The bread was warm and yeasty. Devon chewed and
swallowed. "Thanks," she said ungraciously.

Jared had already caught the attention of the nearest
waiter. Her scallops were removed, replaced by a cup of
clear consommé. "Try that," Jared said. "Works won-
ders."

She stared into the fragile china bowl; he'd engineered
the exchange with ruthless efficiency. Her heart beating like
a triphammer and her hands cold as ice, she glanced over
at him. "What you want you get," she said. "Pronto."

"Drink your soup."

"Just don't ever want me…okay?"

"Do what I say, Devon."

"You don't hear anything that doesn't suit you, do you?" she retorted, fumbled for her spoon and took a mouthful of soup. It was delicious, warming her all the way down her throat to her stomach. She took another mouthful, noticing out of the corner of her eye that Benson was fully occupied with his bride and the guests were enjoying the scallops. She said, "Jared, you tried to buy off my mother."

"Yeah."

He hadn't even bothered denying it. Shaken by sudden fury, Devon said, "That was a loathsome thing to do."

"Eminently practical, I'd say. And I don't know why you're complaining—it didn't work."

"Some women can't be bought—did you get the message?"

"No...only that she's angling for more." His lip curled. "Divorce can be lucrative when you're in my league."

Devon took another mouthful of soup. "You really are despicable."

"Not by my standards. I've learned something in my thirty-eight years, Devon. Everyone can be bought. All women have their price—some higher than others." He stabbed a scallop. "Most of the time, of course, you don't get what you pay for."

"That's because you're paying for it," Devon flashed.

"Haven't you realized yet that everything comes with a price tag?"

She thought of Steve and Peter, and said more sharply than she'd intended, "Of course I have. But your mistake is to equate the price tag with money. Hard cash. Instead of with emotion."

"For a while I thought...but you're really no different from the rest."

She gave him a cool smile. "You realize you've just paid me a compliment?"

His own smile was reluctant. "Solidarity with the sister-hood? You're quick-witted, I'll give you that."

"My goodness—two compliments. Watch out, Jared, you're mellowing before my eyes."

"Good. So you'll like it when I kiss you."

Soup slopped out of her spoon. Carefully Devon replaced the spoon in the bowl. "Are you trying to make Lise jealous? Is that what this is all about?"

"Leave Lise out of this," he rapped, his jaw hardening.

It was a very formidable jaw. Devon retorted, "So you value fidelity as little as emotion."

"You're making a lot of assumptions that are none of your business."

"Fine," she said tartly. "Just as long as you remember that I'm none of your business. Literally. Because that's all women are to you—a business deal."

"The so-called battle of the sexes is one big business deal."

"I couldn't agree less!"

"Darling," Alicia said, "didn't you like your scallops?"

Very much aware that her cheeks were pink with temper and her eyes blazing with emotion—that word again—Devon said hastily, "Not on top of champagne, Mother."

"Benson and I were just saying how much we hope 'The Oaks' will see the arrival of some grandchildren," Alicia said archly; tact had never been her strongest suit.

"Oh...really?" Devon said weakly.

"I do wish you'd change jobs, darling. Jared, she's never home. How can you fall in love when you spend all your time in Borneo and Arabia and Timbuktu?"

"Mother, I've never even been to Timbuktu."

"Don't be so literal-minded, Devon—you know what I mean."

"I enjoy my job," Devon said. "And if I was meant to fall in love, I'm sure I could do it in Arabia just as well as in Toronto."

"You can't develop a relationship in between airports!"

Her mother was serious. Devon said artlessly, "Then I guess you'll have to depend on Jared for the grandchildren."

Benson said, "Unfortunately, Jared doesn't believe in commitment...Lise looked very charming, by the way."

"It's all these careers," Alicia said crossly. "In my day, women stayed home."

Devon bit hard on her lip. Alicia had made a career out of marriage and had stayed in any number of homes, although this was scarcely the appropriate time to say so. One waiter removed her soup; another put a plate of pork medallions in front of her. As her stomach lurched uneasily, she started asking Benson about his horses, and soon they were safely launched. The rest of the dinner, the speeches, the obligatory kissing of the bride by the groom, all passed by her in a blur. As soon as she was released from the head table she sought out Jared's cousin Patrick; he introduced her to some of his friends and for the first time since the wedding had begun Devon started to enjoy herself.

They were laughingly exchanging horror stories about overseas travel when Devon saw Jared striding toward them: tall and commanding, wrapped in an aura of power and sexual charisma that made her deeply wary. The man of danger, she thought with an inner shiver, and wished him a thousand miles away.

He said abruptly, "The dancing's getting underway, Devon—we're expected to lead off after Dad and Alicia."

Dance with Jared? She'd rather march barefoot through the desert. "I'll be along in a minute."

"They want us now."

Short of making a scene, what choice did she have?

Devon said, "Be sure you ask me to dance, Patrick," and swept past Jared, her head held high.

As she crossed the grass, he put an arm hard around her waist; the contact scorched through her silk gown. He said tersely, "Two more hours and this shindig'll be over. Can't be too soon for me."

Or for me, thought Devon.

Dusk had fallen; the dance tent, a ghostly white under the tall elm trees, was entwined with ivy and scented with baskets of roses. Inside, scores of tiny lights sparkled like stars. For a moment Devon relaxed in the circle of Jared's arm, forgetting that she despised him and that a minute ago she also had been longing for the wedding to be over. "Oh, Jared, it's enchanting," she whispered, and twisted in his arms, her smile as vivid as a child's.

His mouth tightened. "Let's dance," he said.

He took her in his arms as though she had some kind of communicable disease. He was a skillful dancer, his steps perfectly in time with the music as they circled Benson and Alicia, and Devon hated every minute of it. When the waltz ended, there was a smattering of applause from the assembled guests. Devon said flatly, "Duty done. Thank you."

"The next one we're dancing for us."

"There isn't any us!"

The orchestra was playing a slow and dreamy melody; as Devon tried to pull free, Jared tightened his hold on her, pulling her to stand body to body, her breasts soft against the wall of his chest. Then he rested his cheek on her hair and in the semi-darkness began to sway to the music.

Her face was nestled in the hollow between his shoulder and his throat; she could smell, very subtly, his aftershave, and, even more subtly, the clean, masculine scent of his skin. His hand slid down to hold her by the hips; his other hand was clasping hers. Nothing in the world could have prevented the flood of desire, sweet and hot and urgent, that swept over Devon.

She wanted this man. Wanted to lie with him, skin to skin, naked bodies entwined. Wanted to travel with him the many roads of passion. Her heartbeat quickened; she was achingly conscious of the thrust of his erection that said more clearly than words that desire was mutual.

She hated everything he stood for. How could she even think of going to bed with him?

With a little moan of dismay she tried to push away from him. But as though her movements excited him, Jared took her chin in his strong fingers and bent his head to kiss her.

As if a spell had been cast over her, Devon waited, letting her lids drift shut as she felt the first light pressure of his lips. To her surprise, there was no anger in his kiss, simply the need—or so she felt—to give her pleasure. Scarcely aware of what she was doing, she looped her arms around his neck, offering her mouth gladly to the warmth of his. He muttered something that she didn't catch, then his tongue swept the soft curve of her lower lip, dipping deeper as she opened to him.

Between one instant and the next, desire was engulfed in a passion so fierce and so primitive that Devon began to tremble. Jared's arm tightened around her waist; for a few brief seconds that could have been hours, he plundered all the sweetness of her mouth. Then, slowly, he lifted his head.

His eyes were as dark as pits; Devon had no idea what he was thinking. He was a stranger to her, she thought in utter panic. Not only a stranger: an enemy. Yet she had allowed him intimacies that she rarely allowed anyone.

She had to end this. Now. In a voice that was almost steady she said, "That'll teach me to drink champagne."

His lashes flickered; dark lashes, she thought abstractedly, as black as his hair. He grated, "You'd only kiss me if you were drunk? Is that what you're telling me?"

Momentarily his arms were lax around her. Devon stepped back, smoothing her hair. "Let's not kid ourselves, Jared—you don't like me and I don't like you. I've had less than four hours' sleep in the last couple of days, and weddings—especially my mother's weddings—are guaranteed to push all my buttons. You go find Lise and I'll ask Patrick to dance with me."

"So that's what you're after? Some guy you can lead around by the nose?"

"I want someone who won't crawl all over me like a starving mongrel!"

"You know what you need? Taming, Devon Fraser—"

"Are you trying to tell me that any woman with the guts to say no to you needs fixing?"

"—and I'm the man to do it."

"Go tame Lise! Go tame any other woman on this dance floor who's stupid enough to get within ten feet of you! But don't you dare talk about taming me, as though I'm some kind of a pink poodle that's up for grabs. You're just not used to a woman saying no. It's a very simple word. One syllable, two letters—I don't know why you have such a problem with it." Briefly she paused for breath. "Thank heavens, there's Patrick. Goodbye, Jared. It's been most instructive meeting you. And you can bet your bottom dollar that this is the year I'll be spending Christmas in Antarctica."

She marched off the dance floor toward the table where Patrick and his friends had ensconced themselves with three bottles of wine and a candle whose flame wavered in the summer breeze. They were all delighted to see her. When next she looked around, Jared was nowhere to be seen. Good riddance, she thought, and hoped her mother and his

father had been too wrapped up in each other to see the
way she'd kissed Jared.

For the briefest of moments Jared contemplated going after
Devon. Seizing her in his arms, regardless of the wedding
guests, and kissing her into submission in the middle of the
dance floor. Because he could. He knew it. He'd felt her
delicious surrender through the whole length of his body:
so sudden and so complete.

She wanted him just as much as he wanted her.

So why was he standing all by himself on the dance
floor?

Was she an extremely clever tactician, dishing out just
enough of her sexual lures to keep him interested and then
removing herself? There were words for that kind of behavior, very crude words. Or did she really want nothing
to do with him?

Christmas in Antarctica. Dammit, she'd liked being
kissed by him! He'd swear to it on every fence post on his
father's land.

Tension thrummed in his shoulders. His fists, he realized,
were clenched at his sides, and a few of the guests were
starting to eye him curiously. Jared let out his breath in a
long swoosh and went in search of Lise.

He'd been avoiding Lise, no question of it. But when he
approached the group of which she was part she greeted
him with her usual provocative smile, and it would have
taken a keener ear than his to detect any annoyance in her
voice.

She was a very good actress. And he knew for sure she
was interested in him. He'd swear to that on a whole stack
of Bibles.

Grimly he strove to enjoy himself, but it was as though
Devon was hovering beside him in her turquoise gown the
whole time, listening to every platitude, counting how

many times Lise called him darling. A word he hated, he decided with the calm of extreme rage. Alicia used that particular endearment for Devon all the time.

Would he ever forget Devon's childlike pleasure when she'd seen the dance tent? What had she called it? Enchanting?

If she'd faked that, she was the one who should be playing on Broadway. Not Lise.

Enchanting. It was he who'd been enchanted, Jared thought with an honesty he couldn't gainsay. He'd intended, when he'd kissed Devon's hand, that it be the equivalent of her turquoise dress: a slap in the face. But when he'd kissed her on the dance floor he'd forgotten all about teaching her a lesson. All he'd wanted to do was seduce her.

Lise tugged at his sleeve and Jared struggled to pay attention to what everyone was saying. But, in spite of himself, his thoughts kept marching on. When he met a new woman, one he desired, he always felt very much in control of the situation. He knew all the moves: they'd never failed him. He always got what he wanted, and he got it on his own terms.

He could have Lise on his terms. Any time he liked.

Maybe that was why he didn't want her.

Despite the fact that they'd been dating for the last couple of years, he'd never once gone to bed with her. There'd always been a reason for delaying that particular move—a sudden trip to inspect a resort in Kenya, a crisis in the Canadian oil fields, a slump in the stock market. Excuses, he thought savagely. Excuses to hide the uncomfortable truth that what was so easily achieved wasn't worth having.

He could remember very clearly the night Lise had made her move. What instinct had warned him that she'd be as adept and passionless in bed as she was manipulative out of it? He didn't know. But she'd been so sure of seducing him that his refusal to become her lover had shocked her. She'd recovered fast; he had almost been able to watch her inwardly balancing the Holt millions against sexual rejection, and opting for the money. Broadway fame was fickle, and she had no aptitude for movies. Lise wanted the security—both financial and social—that his fortune would bring her. So now she was biding her time: waiting with supreme confidence for him to change his mind.

Since he'd met Devon, it seemed highly unlikely he would. Devon wasn't easy, like Lise. Devon had a fiery temper that she didn't bother to hide and a tongue that could scour splinters from teak.

A body to die for.

She'd told him she didn't want his money.

Sure, he thought. No one, but no one, was immune to the amount of money at his disposal.

The sooner he forgot about Devon Fraser, the better.

With new determination he danced with Lise and all the other women in their party; he made sure a large bundle of tin cans was tied to the bumper of the limo that was to take Benson and Alicia to Toronto for the night, and he waved goodbye as they left. Letting his eyes slide over Devon as if she were just another guest, he bent his head to listen to Lise.

"Darling," she was saying, "would you mind if I stayed here overnight? I dread the drive back with the Westons; he's such a bore."

Jared said easily, "Better not, Lise. I've got to be up with the birds in the morning. I'm taking the early flight to Tokyo."

For a moment he would have sworn he saw pure fury in her pale blue eyes, but with the tiniest of pouts she replied, "Whatever you say. But we see so little of each other..."

"I'll be back in four or five days."

"Dinner at the Plaza on Friday," she said, "our usual

table,'' and stood on tiptoes to give him a lingering kiss on the mouth.

He felt absolutely nothing. A big fat zero.

What the devil was wrong with him? Any number of men would give their eye teeth to be kissed by the beautiful Lise Lamont of Broadway fame. But all he felt was a ferocious impatience for her to be gone.

It took him ten minutes to maneuver her and the Westons into their Lincoln and see them off down the driveway. Then several other guests cornered him. Jared detached himself as quickly as he could and found himself jogging toward the dance tent. The band was playing hard rock and the remaining guests were settling in for the duration. Devon was nowhere to be seen.

He stood very still. His heart was pounding in his chest and his gut was churning. Neither of these symptoms had anything to do with his jog across the grass. Was it lust he was suffering from? Rage that she should have disappeared? Or an ugly combination of the two?

Patrick and his buddies looked as though they were set for the rest of the night—Patrick tended to party hard on his rare visits to civilization. Jared went up to him. "Have you seen Devon?"

Patrick looked around vaguely. "Last I saw she was dancing with Gerry. Sorry, ol' man."

Jared made the rounds of the other tents, knowing as he did so that his search was hopeless. Devon had had almost no sleep for the better part of two days and the wedding was virtually over. She'd gone to her room. And why should she bother to speak to him first? They'd done nothing but fight since the moment they'd met.

Stray cats had nothing on him and Devon.

He was damned if he was going to knock on her door like a lovesick adolescent. Besides, if she was on the other side of it, he'd want to knock it down.

Maybe she'd gone back to Toronto. Away from "The Oaks" altogether. After all, she'd said goodbye to him on the dance floor. Goodbye. As if it had happened only moments ago, he could remember how her blue eyes had blazed like the opal on her breast.

He ran for the front door, his palms ice-cold. Her red Mazda was still parked in the driveway. For a moment Jared leaned his hand on the smooth red hood, as though the contact could tell him something about its owner. Then, with a gesture of self-disgust, he stripped off his bow tie and took the front steps two at a time.

CHAPTER FOUR

DEVON blew her nose on a tissue she'd found in the pocket of her jeans, scrubbed the tears from her cheeks on the sleeve of her ribbed shirt and gave the mare's forehead one last rub. "Thanks, old girl," she whispered. The mare tossed her head, then nuzzled at Devon's fingers.

At the barn door Devon said a soft word of thanks to the security guard, who'd let her in due to her status as Benson's new stepdaughter. "Goodnight."

"Night, miss."

She could still hear the echo of music from the garden. For a moment she leaned on the fence, gazing unseeingly at the neatly raked show ring. Ever since her mother's third marriage, to Bertram, the British earl, Devon had found true comfort in the company of horses. Those were the years she'd been sent to that horrible day school, where her Canadian accent and her lack of sophistication had made her the target of everything from teasing to ostracism. But in the evenings the earl's head groomsman had taught her the intricacies of dressage and the sheer joy of showjumping, both of which she'd taken to by instinct. More importantly, he'd taught her to treat each horse as an individual with something to say to her.

It was the horses who'd kept her sane those four years, until the earl had dumped her mother for a Swedish heiress and she and Alicia had moved to Texas to live with the oilman. There she'd learned a very different style of riding. But the horses had been the same, offering her companionship in the face of what she now realized had been a long-term, crushing loneliness.

Tonight, after she'd left the tent, too exhausted to think of sleep, she'd stripped off her turquoise dress, changed into jeans and fled to the stables for the simple comfort of the scent of hay and the touch of noses sleek as velvet. She didn't know why she'd cried.

It was everything to do with weddings and nothing to do with Jared.

She straightened, knowing she was still too restless to go indoors. But she wasn't going to start thinking about Jared Holt. No way. So what if his sexual expertise had dissolved all her defences? Not to mention her knees. His attitude toward women in general, and toward her mother and herself in particular, gave her the creeps. Shoving her hands in her pockets, she wandered toward the rose garden, whose clustered blooms scented the air seductively. A few more minutes of solitude and she'd be ready to settle for the night.

"So there you are."

Devon whirled, watching a man detach himself from the ancient rhododendrons that flanked the white-painted barn. Jared. Of course. Still in his black trousers and crisp white shirt, now minus tie and open at the throat. A light from the end of the barn illuminated his sculpted features. She said sharply, "I'm tired...I'm going indoors."

"You're going the wrong way."

She hated the mockery in his voice. "Jared," she said carefully, "do you ever see a woman as a person?"

"Turning all touchy-feely on me, Devon?"

"Not very likely."

He stepped closer. "You've been to the barn."

It was her turn for mockery. "Do I smell of horses? Sorry about that...I'm sure Givenchy is more to your taste."

He was standing so close to her now that she could have

reached out and touched him. He said roughly, "You've been crying."

"I haven't!"

He suddenly looked murderous. "Did someone do something to hurt you?"

She said shrewishly, "Your father married my mother. Isn't that enough?"

"I wish to God you'd drop this holier-than-thou attitude that you've got a soul above money!"

"And I wish you'd look further than your bank account! Or do you depend on it to prop up your masculinity?"

"Lay off, Devon," he said with menacing quietness.

She tossed her head. "Hitting too close to home?"

He ticked off on his fingers. "We both know how you responded to me on the dance floor. You despise my money—or so you say. Therefore in your eyes my so-called masculinity must be separate from my bank account. Come on, Devon, you can't have it both ways."

"Oh, logic," she said irritably. "You and the Greeks. Come to think of it, you and Aristotle share much the same opinion of women. Animalistic airheads."

To her annoyance, Jared was laughing at her. "So much for the greatest philosopher who ever lived. I'll tell you one thing—you don't bore me."

"Gee, thanks."

He looked younger and devastatingly attractive when he laughed, Devon thought uneasily, and was seized with the sudden desire to make him laugh again. Subduing it, she heard him say, "I've got an idea—a perfect antidote to too much wedding."

She said moodily, "Fifth time lucky? I wonder what the odds are?"

"Is your mother the reason you have a job that doesn't allow for commitment?"

"Do you turn into a shrink after midnight?"

He laughed a second time, his teeth very white. "You didn't ask what my idea was."

"I'm scared to," she said, scowling at him.

"It's very simple. I'm starving. Too much puff pastry and wedding cake—I could do with a good old-fashioned hamburger. What do you say we raid the kitchen?"

Her lips quirked. "Are you serious?"

"Yes, ma'am." He took her by the hand. "Come along."

Devon liked the feel of his palm against hers, and in the leather thongs she'd bought in a bazaar in Delhi she was much shorter than he, which also filled her with an obscure excitement. But she wouldn't get into any trouble making hamburgers. There was something very asexual about ground beef.

He led her past the barn through a side door of the house, then down a passageway into a kitchen that was like an elaborate warehouse for fancy equipment. "Your mother," Jared said, "plans to put up frilly curtains."

"My mother loves frills," Devon responded gloomily. "You should have seen Dunton Castle by the time we left."

"Lace on the portcullis?"

"And gingham on the dungeon door... You know what? I'm hungry, too—where do you keep the onions?"

The hamburgers were delicious. Jared, like herself, liked them smothered with relish, peppers and ketchup, and dripping with melted cheese. Devon took her last bite and gave a sigh of repletion. "My cholesterol count's probably hitting the roof and I feel a great deal better."

Jared had splattered grease on his shirtfront. Somehow that made him a lot more human. And he hadn't once tried to touch her in the last hour. So Devon just grinned when he reached over with a piece of paper towel and said, "Hold still—ketchup on your chin."

"Only ketchup?"

His eyes intent, he scrubbed at her jaw. Then, as if he couldn't help himself, he ran his finger along the soft curve of her mouth. "You're so beautiful," he said huskily.

Now was her chance to run, Devon thought wildly, and mumbled, "I had five minutes to pack—these are my oldest jeans and my hair's a wreck."

Taking his time, Jared looked her up and down. Her hair was indeed falling out of its pins. Her ribbed sweater hugged her breasts and her high-arched feet were bare in their worn sandals. He said, "You could wear a feed bag and you'd look ten times better than anyone else at the wedding."

"When you look at me like that, I melt...just like the cheese," Devon said unsteadily.

"You taste much better than cheddar," he said and pulled her to her feet, kissing her until she whimpered with pleasure in his arms and any thought of running away had vanished, lost in the flames of a passion she'd never known she was capable of. She kissed him back, feeling him cup her breast under her sweater, longing for the more intimate touch of flesh on flesh. Then, suddenly, Jared swung her up into his arms and pushed his way through the kitchen's swing door.

Against her right knee she could feel the thudding of his heart. She had, instinctively, put her arms around his neck; the hair at his nape was as silky as she'd thought it would be. Fighting back the urge to stroke it, she sputtered, "Jared—put me down."

He was now climbing a set of stairs she hadn't seen before. "Watch your elbows," he grunted.

"Put me down, I said—where are we going?"

"Where do you think? To bed."

"We can't do that!"

"We sure can. What's to stop us?"

She wriggled in his grip, feeling as impotent as a fish on a hook. "For starters, we don't like each other."

"You'll like what we do together," he said confidently.

He was now striding down a long hallway, lined with a set of old hunting prints. It must be a different wing of the house, Devon thought confusedly. "We aren't going to—"

"Nearly there," he said, fumbling with the handle of the end door. It swung open onto a suite of rooms that overlooked fenced meadows and the black bulk of the distant forest. Jared pushed the door shut and put her down, sliding his hands down her arms and searching out her mouth as though he could brook no delay. He kissed her with an intensity that made Devon's head swim, his tongue dancing with hers, his hands traveling the length of her spine, up and down, in a hypnotic rhythm that filled her with pleasure.

Unconsciously she arched toward him, looping her arms around his neck. He whispered against her lips, "Tell me you want me, Devon."

Very slowly, she drew back. Standing tall, she said, "Of course I want you. But—"

"I want you, too...more than I can say. Tonight is for us, Devon. No yesterday. No tomorrow. Just tonight."

Slowly Devon let her eyes wander over his face, wondering if she looked hard enough, deeply enough, she could somehow fathom this man who compelled her toward him yet was so much an unknown, frightening, and hostile quantity. He bore her gaze steadily, without smiling, giving nothing away.

Go to bed with him, a little voice whispered in her ear. What better way to get to know a man?

Run a mile, said another voice. You swore off intimacy seven years ago, and Peter didn't make you change your mind. Okay, so Jared's a hunk and your blood's in an up-

roar. Hormones, Devon. Estrogen meets up with testoster-
one. Nature's way of making sure sex never goes obsolete.

Jared's hands were still resting on her shoulders, their
warmth spreading irresistibly through her body. He was
standing so close to her she could count his individual
lashes; she found him utterly desirable. When had she ever
felt such a storm of passion from one kiss? Such raw hunger, such desperation? Despite all her travels, she'd lived—
her eyes widened at the insight—very safely ever since
Steve had so grievously deceived her. No risks. Always in
control of her sexuality. Never letting anything—or rather,
anyone—get out of hand.

Peter would certainly agree with her. She'd never gone
to bed with Peter.

But Jared Holt had broken through all those boundaries.

As though he was impatient with her silence, Jared said
forcefully, "I'll be good to you, I swear."

"And if I choose to leave right now, will you try and
stop me?"

"Force has never been my specialty."

If he'd been any other man, Devon would have sworn
she'd hurt him with her question. But the idea was ludicrous with someone as well armored as Jared. She said with
stubborn pride, "I am not after your money."

The pulse throbbing at the base of his throat, Jared said,
"This is about sex, Devon. Nothing more than sex—I
meant it when I said there'll be no tomorrow—but certainly
nothing less. I think Aunt Bessie hit on something—we
strike sparks in each other. I don't know why. I don't really
care. But believe me, I'm not usually this unsubtle."

With a flicker of unwilling respect, because he was being
brutally honest, Devon stood very still. She could choose.
That was what he was saying.

He was like the tiger she'd seen padding through the
shadows in the jungle near Bengal: untameable, calling to

her in some elemental way. One thing he was not, and that was safe.

Somehow she knew she had her answer. She was sick to death of safety. It had taken a meeting with a man with hair as black as night to show her that truth.

Devon reached up and with her fingertips very deliberately traced the hard jut of Jared's cheekbones, the taut line of his jaw, the warmth of his lips; her face was intent as she allowed the astonishing intimacy of this exploration to heat her blood. Then, burying her hands in his hair, she drew his head down and kissed him with a boldness she hadn't known was hers.

For a moment she felt his utter stillness, as though at some profound level she'd taken him by surprise. Then he took her in his arms, fiercely and possessively, like a man who's waited too long to fulfill a need as basic as food or air. Their kiss deepened as they strained toward each other, Devon making tiny sounds of pleasure deep in her throat as she opened to him with a generosity that, she dimly sensed, she'd trammeled for years.

Jared lifted his head; with some of her own intensity, he searched for the pins in her hair, drawing them out one by one until her blond curls, rich and shiny, tumbled to her shoulders. He eased her sweater over her head and undid the catch on her bra, tossing it to the floor. Then, watching the play of expression on her face, he touched her breasts through the shining fall of her hair, stroking them to their peaks, teasing her nipples to hardness.

Her breathing quickened. In the pale moonlight that filtered through the windows his eyes were depthless; she could lose herself in them, thought Devon, and never find herself again. Stifling terror before it could be born, she began undoing the buttons on his shirt. She spread the fabric apart to bare the dark hair curling on his chest, and tangled her fingers in it, the heat of his skin making her blood race in her veins. With sudden impatience he yanked the shirt free of his waistband; it joined her garments on the floor. Devon stepped closer, rubbing her nipples against him, briefly closing her eyes in ecstasy.

She felt him cup one breast and take it in his mouth, his tongue laving her until she wondered if she could die from sheer delight. With all her strength she held him to her, feeling the hardness of bone beneath his hair, dropping her cheek to rest there. Her whole body felt suffused with sweetness and with incredible promise; Jared, she already knew, had no intention of rushing his seduction of her.

For seduction it was. Never in her life had she been so gloriously and sensually fondled. Knowing herself beautiful in his eyes, shamelessly hungry for each and every caress, Devon was filled with the longing to give Jared as much delight as she was receiving. They had time, she thought, all the time in the world for a lovemaking she already knew would be beyond anything she'd ever experienced; pierced by desire, she watched the muscles ripple in his shoulders as he raised his head.

This time he found the zipper on her jeans, sliding the faded denim from her thighs until she was clad only in a pair of lacy briefs. Her cheeks flushed as with excruciating slowness he slid his palms along the taut curve of her waist to the rise of her buttocks, pressing her against his erection.

"Come to bed with me, Devon," he said huskily, and for the second time lifted her in his arms.

Her cheek lay against his chest; she murmured, "I want this to last forever, and I want you inside me so badly I can hardly breathe."

He'd carried her into a bedroom whose tall windows were filled with the myriad restless shadows of leaves in the moonlight. Then she was on the bed and he was lying on top of her, kissing her closed lids, her throat, her breasts, as though his one need was to imprint himself on her, to touch every inch of her body. With one hand he drew the scrap of lace down her legs, then, with exquisite gentleness, he parted her thighs, teasing the warm, wet petals of her flesh until she writhed beneath his touch.

Desperate to be filled by him, Devon reached for the waistband of his trousers; moments later he was naked to her. With the first shyness she'd shown, she whispered, ''You're so beautiful...''

''Touch me, Devon,'' he said, guiding her hand down his corded belly to the hot silkiness of his manhood.

She curled her hand round him, watching his face convulse, and suddenly knew she had no need of shyness. Not now. Not with Jared. In a single lithe movement she straddled him, then lowered herself until he slid within her, clasped by her tight, sleek warmth. He thrust upward; she gasped his name and rode him, her head falling forward until her long hair almost hid her breasts, aware with every nerve-ending she possessed of Jared grasping her by the hips.

Still holding her, he rolled so they lay face to face. ''This is too fast,'' he muttered. ''I want you to—''

She wrapped her thighs around him in a frantic longing to have him as deeply inside her as it was possible. ''No...no, now, Jared,'' she whimpered. ''Now...please.''

Her words were like a catalyst. He thrust again and again, their rhythms inexorably meeting in an explosion of sensation unlike anything Devon had ever experienced. She cried out his name, and with an all-encompassing joy felt the throb of his release. Wrapping her arms around him, holding him as tightly as she could, she closed her eyes, and heard the pounding of his heart inseparable from the racing of her own.

Until two shall become one flesh...

She knew what that meant now. Knew it in her bones. How strange that she'd had to wait so long to find out.

"Devon," Jared said unsteadily, "are you okay?"

She opened her eyes. His chest was still heaving; there was a faint sheen of sweat on his forehead. "Okay?" she quavered. "Nope."

"It's been a long time. I was too—"

In a surge of what was undoubtedly tenderness, she chuckled, "Okay, you say? Not the right word, Jared. I feel miles beyond okay. I feel marvellously and wonderfully ravished." And with wicked provocation she stretched as gracefully as a cat, linked her hands behind his neck and kissed him very thoroughly.

He responded most satisfactorily; so much so that Devon realized she was all too ready to be ravished a second time. Nibbling at his lower lip, she said with artless enthusiasm, "We could do it again. If you like."

"Oh, I like." He grinned, a boyish grin that sent another of those disconcerting waves of tenderness through her. "Had it been a while for you, too?"

"A very long while." Like seven years.

He shifted so he lay on top of her, keeping most of his weight on his elbows. "So you want to do it again, do you, Devon Fraser?"

She ran her palms down the long curve of his spine, tracing the small bumps of his vertebrae, then the taut rise of his buttocks. "I know you're ready," she said naughtily.

"Can't hide that." His smile faded, and as though the words were dragged from him, he said, "You make me feel as though I've never done this before...what is it about you that's so different from anyone else?"

Devon didn't want to think about any other women in Jared's arms. The women of his past, the women of his future. Intuitively she pressed her fingers to his lips. "No talk," she whispered. "We don't need words. For one night we belong to each other, Jared. Just one night. Make love to me...and let me make love to you."

"There's nothing I want more," he said throatily, and, with the lightest of kisses, closed her lids. Her nerves attuned to an excruciating sensitivity, she felt the featherlight touch of his lips on her face, her throat, the hollows of her collarbone; and the whole time she was repetitively roaming the hard planes of his back and shoulders, memorizing them, her nostrils filled with the scent of his body and of their loving.

How could this not be loving?

With a fierce concentration, as though she was unutterably precious to him, Jared played with the silken rise of her breasts until her hips were twisting beneath him and her small, broken cries spoke of pleasure and pain. When he lifted her, she went trustingly to his embrace, and when he carried her across the room, then put her down and held her against him in front of the big mirror on the bathroom door, Devon saw a woman she hadn't known existed: a glowing creature whose pale limbs were eclipsed by Jared's tanned muscularity, his height, his purely male triumph in his possession of her. She watched him cup her breasts, bury his face in her hair, and trembled with primitive hunger.

Turning in his arms, Devon kissed him until she could scarcely breathe. Then, in the mirror, she saw him slide his mouth down her body, past her taut nipples, her belly, to the juncture of her thighs. Throwing back her head, she cried out his name, lost to the sweet madness of surrender.

But before she could tumble into the abyss he lifted her, to lie on top of him on the bed again. He must have felt the frantic thrumming of her heart, seen her dazzled eyes: she had no wish to hide anything from him. With an inarticulate groan, he kissed her fingers and then her mouth, his hair black against the pillow.

Loving the roughness of his body hair against her breasts and thighs, Devon began her own slow, sensual exploration, sensing how openly Jared was allowing her the freedom to his body. He was a proud and private man; she'd known that from the beginning. His vulnerability was a gift.

She could not possibly have abused such a gift; she only craved to enjoy it to the uttermost and to return it to him the best way she could. Her hands, her mouth and all the graceful curves of her body were her own gift to him; with them, she sought to arouse in him the peaks of pleasure that he'd shown her. The arrowed hair at his navel led her further; very gently she took him in her mouth, heard him gasp.

He lifted her again, and, covering her with his big body, he thrust deep within her. She'd never seen such blazing intensity in a man's face. If he was conqueror, he was also conquered, she realized with an atavistic thrill of pride. As, of course, was she. Then, inexorably, Devon felt her own rhythms rise to meet his, and again tumbled from ecstasy to the ancient and limitless peace of release.

Gradually Jared's harsh breathing quietened, the heavy pounding of his heart slowing against her ribcage. They were equals, she and Jared, Devon thought with distant certainty. Equals. True partners. Holding him in her arms even as she was held, she closed her eyes and let herself drift into the sleep of satiation and fulfillment.

CHAPTER FIVE

WHEN Devon woke, it was still dark. She lay very still, watching the leaves dancing in the moonlight, and for a few seconds had no idea where she was.

Then she noticed other things: the jut of a man's hip, the weight and warmth of his thigh over her own, the fan of his breath on her cheek. Her arm was lying loosely over his ribcage, which reverberated to the steady beat of his heart.

Jared. She was in bed with Jared.

Her heart dipped in her breast. She was instantly and fully awake, and for a moment could only stare into his sleeping face, as if it might somehow disappear and she'd wake up in her own bed and realize she'd been dreaming.

A dream or a nightmare? she thought crazily.

She'd gone to bed on the strength of a few hours' acquaintance with a man who despised all women, and in particular Devon and Alicia, as money-grabbing opportunists. A man who was, officially, her stepbrother, even though they weren't related by blood. A man she would be required to meet and be on outwardly friendly terms with for as long as her mother's fifth marriage lasted.

Devon swallowed a spurt of near-hysterical laughter. For once, she was on the side of divorce. The sooner the better. How could she have been so stupid, so criminally short-sighted?

So wanton?

She dared not start dwelling on all the things she and Jared had done together, here in this very bed, such a short while ago. She'd be lost if she did.

She had to get out of here. Fast. If Jared woke and kissed her even once, she'd make love with him again. She knew she would.

She inched her leg from under his, and slid her arm free. He didn't stir. Very slowly, she eased her body away from him. He muttered something she couldn't catch. Devon froze, holding her breath. But then he settled again, his breathing resuming its slow, deep rhythm.

Sitting up, her eyes adjusted now to the dim light, Devon could distinguish the tangle of their clothing on the floor, and felt hot color flood her cheeks. As every detail of how her garments had ended up on the carpet raced through her brain, the sweet ache of desire blossomed instantly in her belly.

Stop it, Devon! Stop it. You can't afford to remember the incredible pleasure of making love with Jared. Not now. Not until you're miles away from him and from "The Oaks."

Her feet touched the carpet; she stood up, tiptoed toward her clothes and picked them up. Then, naked, she crept out of the bedroom into the living room. Awkward with haste, she yanked on her sweater and jeans, wincing at the tiny sounds of the zipper, and shoved her feet into her sandals. Clutching her underwear, feeling like a character in a French farce, she turned the door handle and pushed on the door.

It opened soundlessly and closed behind her just as quietly. Devon scurried down the hallway, trying to get her bearings. Instead of taking the stairs to the kitchen, she turned a corner and found herself in another hall that, to her infinite relief, she recognized. Almost tripping in her haste, she ran into her own room and frantically threw everything that was hers into her open suitcase.

Car keys...what had she done with them?

Her hands were ice-cold and for a moment Devon

couldn't even think. But then she saw the keys lying innocently on the bureau, and with a gasp of relief grabbed them and ran for the door. The hall was empty.

She'd been afraid she'd find Jared blocking her way.

She took the stairs at a run, undid the bolts on the front door and slipped through. Her red convertible was sitting exactly where she'd parked it yesterday. Yesterday? It was a lifetime ago. Her case bumping against her leg, she hurried toward it.

"Can I help you, miss?"

Stifling a shriek of alarm, Devon saw a security guard marching toward her, the same one who'd let her into the barn last night. Drawing on every ounce of her coolheadedness, a trait she'd often needed in places like Yemen and Papua New Guinea, Devon said calmly, "Oh, I'm so glad you're here. I have to catch an early flight out of Toronto—I should have left last night, but I'd had one too many glasses of champagne. Will I need a pass to leave the property?"

"I'll give the guy at the gate a buzz," he said easily, "and tell him you're Mr. Holt's stepdaughter."

"Thanks."

"Safe journey, miss."

At the big wrought-iron gates, Devon waved at another guard and accelerated onto the country road. She was a very good driver and she'd have the roads to herself.

There was no sign of any pursuit.

Two hours later, after a fast and uneventful drive, Devon was unlocking the door of her sixteenth-floor condo on Queen's Quay. Stepping inside, she snapped the bolt, put the chain in its slot and dropped her case.

She was home. She was safe.

Alicia and Benson were leaving for a Greek cruise today; if her mother phoned, she'd tell her under no circumstances to give Jared her address or phone number. In a couple of days she herself was leaving for Chile.

As a crushing exhaustion settled on her, Devon lugged her case into her bedroom and switched on the light. Her room was painted sage-green with white trim, the bed had white covers and heaps of white cushions, and her desk and bedside table were bleached pine. The picture windows overlooked Lake Ontario and the Toronto Islands.

Home. Safe.

She sank down slowly on the bed. Why had she been so terrified that Jared would follow her? Race after her along the country roads in the middle of the night? It would be the last thing he'd do. One night, he'd said. No tomorrow. He'd said something else: that it was only sex between them. No more. No less.

She was the one who inwardly had labeled their wild, impulsive night together as lovemaking.

Her cheeks scorched with shame, Devon knew there were other words that could be used of the short time she'd spent in Jared's bed. A one-night stand. An easy lay. She pressed her palms to her face, wishing with all her heart she could erase the last twelve hours. Why, oh, why hadn't she stayed in Yemen? Then she'd never have met him and, under the stress of her mother's wedding and her own exhaustion, fallen into bed with him. Fallen like a ripe plum from a tree.

She'd cheapened herself, betrayed all her principles, because a black-haired man with such menacing and beautiful grace had kissed her and carried her off to his bed.

How could you, Devon? How could you?

Jared woke to the first low rays of the sun slanting across his bed. The sheets were twisted around his hips; he was cold. Swiftly he reached out for Devon, wanting her body pressed to his in all its delicious warmth and softness.

His outstretched hand found only more crumpled sheets.

He opened his eyes. Apart from himself, the bed was empty.

He sat up with a muttered curse, instantly wide awake. The water wasn't running in the bathroom and the door, the door with the mirror, was ajar, just as it had been last night when he'd exulted in all the voluptuous curves of Devon's body. Her astonishing beauty.

Her clothes were gone.

He flung his legs over the side of the bed, grabbing his trousers and hauling them on, his brain racing. Maybe she'd gone to the kitchen to find something to eat and hadn't wanted to wake him.

That was it. Of course. Watching her eat the hamburger last night, he'd been amused by her appetite: Lise wouldn't be caught dead licking mustard off her fingers.

He strode down the hallway to an unoccupied front bedroom and thrust the sheer curtains aside. Devon's red Mazda was no longer in the driveway.

She'd left. Some time in the middle of the night, she'd gotten out of bed without waking him, and left.

Normally he woke instantly to the slightest sound. But then nothing about last night had been normal.

Jared dropped the curtains back in place. In his bare feet he padded back to his suite of rooms, closing the outer door. There was a hollow ache in the pit of his stomach and all his movements were slow, like those of an older man. A man who'd had a severe and very disagreeable shock.

One night, he'd said to her. There'll be no tomorrow. But he hadn't said half a night. A third of a night, a quarter of a night. How dared she leave before the night was over? Without as much as saying goodbye to him. Then, with another of those disconcerting surges of hope, Jared ran his eyes over the bedside tables and the bureau.

No note. Nothing. Only her absence. A bed empty of her laughter, her brilliant eyes, her exquisite body.

He'd never in his life had his control so swept away by a woman as he had last night. He'd forgotten every one of his rules, all the careful steps by which he usually orchestrated a seduction. Raking his fingers through his hair, he admitted with another clenching of his belly that Devon had stripped him of more than his clothing; she'd removed his restraint, his power, his long-cultivated detachment.

From the minute he'd seen her in that turquoise dress he'd resolved to possess her. He hadn't, however, thought beyond possession. He'd never had to before, so why would he have done so yesterday?

He'd even talked, in the heat of anger, about taming her. But to have used such a word when Devon had lain in his arms would have been an obscenity. Both of them had behaved with a wildness that, for him at least, was totally out of character.

How could he know what Devon was like with anyone else? She was an unknown quantity, a woman he hadn't even met twenty-four hours ago.

He'd also wanted revenge. As clearly as though she were in front of him, he could remember Devon's small smile of triumph when he'd first seen her in that glorious dress. So had he carried her to his bed solely from motives of revenge? In the cool morning light, Jared didn't think so. He'd taken her to bed because he hadn't been able to help himself.

Because he'd liked her.

His jaw dropped. Liked her? He'd lusted after her, that was all.

Both, he thought slowly. Her intelligence had invigorated him, her temper had sparked his own, her sense of humor had amused him. Genuine liking coupled with a depth of passion new to him.

He must have been out of his mind.

Yeah, he thought. Now you're getting close. You were out of your mind, your famous, analytical, cold-blooded mind. Devon Fraser bewitched you. Seduced you. Enchanted you. And the revenge, if he was to use that word, had been hers when he'd woken to an empty bed.

Anger seethed to life, roiling in his chest. She'd used him. Used him and sneaked off in the night without as much as a thank-you-very-much-it-was-nice-meeting-you.

If she was after his money, she was screwing up big time.

Or had she not liked what they'd done together in his big bed? Perhaps he'd bored her so she hadn't wanted to hang around for any repetition. Certainly his technique had been shot to hell. Usually he prided himself on prolonging his seductions, step by step ensuring that his partner received as much pleasure as he was prepared to give; and, of course, he always made sure she was fully satiated.

Technique? With Devon he hadn't had any technique. He'd abandoned himself to a passion that had made nonsense of rules and well-timed moves. Of detachment and restraint.

Perhaps she'd faked all her responses, those broken cries of pleasure, the strength with which she'd held him close. After all, what did he really know about her? It was entirely possible that she took a new lover every week, and discarded each of them just as heartlessly.

But her eyes—those dazzlingly blue eyes—she couldn't have faked the joy and warmth that had shone from them. Could she?

Desperately Jared fought back all the other memories that began flooding back as irrevocably as an ocean tide. Devon's luscious pink-tipped breasts, the inflammatory movements of her hips, the incredible length of her legs... As he rubbed his palms over his face, he suddenly realized that the very scent of her had been absorbed into his hands and his body, and that he wanted her right now just as compulsively as he had last night.

As furious with himself as with Devon, he stalked to the bathroom, stripped off his trousers and stepped under the shower, pummeling his muscles with hot water, then with cold. There, he thought grimly, grabbing the nearest towel. She was gone. The last trace of her.

Now all he had to do was forget her. Put her out of his mind as if he'd never met her, let alone taken her to bed. Although there was one other thing he should do, he thought with angry accuracy: pray that she did indeed go to Antarctica for Christmas.

Ten days later, Jared was sprawled on his leather chester-field in the study of his Upper East Side penthouse, reading the weekly newsletter from a brokerage firm. It was ten p.m. Through the floor-to-ceiling windows overlooking the tree-dark spread of Central Park, shone the lights of Manhattan, more numerous than the stars and bright enough to blank them out. He underlined a couple of sentences, frowning. He'd do well to take that piece of advice, he thought, and frowned more deeply as the phone rang.

Who was calling him at this hour?

It had better not be Lise. He wasn't in the mood for Lise. He'd stuck to his word and taken her to the Plaza last Friday when he'd returned from Tokyo, and subliminally, for the entire evening, he'd wanted her to be Devon.

"Hello?" he said curtly.

"Jared..."

"Dad...so you're back?"

"Got in last night. Had a wonderful time, and Alicia loved Paros and Ikaria."

I bet she did, Jared thought sourly. "Are you at 'The Oaks'? Or staying in Toronto?"

"We're home. Devon's still in Chile, so there was no

point in hanging around Toronto. She gets back Friday night.''

"Chile," Jared repeated noncommittally.

"Yeah…something to do with copper. She flies home via New York. Maybe the two of you could connect.''

No bloody way, thought Jared, and said, "What airline?''

Benson said casually, "I wasn't sure at the wedding if the two of you were hitting it off?''

"Oh, well, you know weddings…right up there on the stress list. It'd be nice to see her, even if it's only at the airport. For the sake of family solidarity and all that.''

I'm turning into one helluva liar, Jared thought, and heard his father say, "Just a sec, then, I'll put Alicia on. She knows all the details… Honey, have a word with Jared, would you?''

"Hello, Jared," Alicia said cautiously.

Jared said heartily, "Hi, Alicia, glad to hear you had a good time. Dad said Devon might be passing through on Friday. Have you any idea when?''

"I've got it right here…I always like to know her itinerary. I worry about her dreadfully in all those awful places; I only wish she'd quit that darn job. Here it is." Alicia reeled off the flight times.

Jared jotted them down, wondering why he was having this conversation. There'd be no secrets with Alicia. Devon would soon know he'd been asking about her. He said with false joviality, "Guess I won't be able to see her…I have tickets for Yo-Yo Ma that night.''

"You do?" Alicia squeaked. "How bizarre! Devon adores cello music, but she was in Borneo when the tickets went on sale and they were all gone by the time she got back. Well, never mind. You and she will have to get together some other time.''

"Do me a favour, then, Alicia? Don't mention it to her. I wouldn't want to disappoint her further."

"You're right, of course," Alicia said, clearly flattered to have been taken into his confidence.

A few minutes later Jared put down the phone. So Devon liked cello music. One more facet to a woman he'd been unable to exorcise from his daytime thoughts or his dreams at night.

He picked up the report again. But ten minutes later he was still reading the same paragraph, not one word of which was making any sense at all.

He tossed the newsletter on the table. The brief time Devon had spent in his bed at "The Oaks" had merely whetted his appetite. He still wanted her. Craved her body night and day. But this time, he thought, he was going to get her on his terms. He'd be in control. He'd be the one to decide when she'd leave.

Last leg of the journey, Devon thought thankfully, smiling at the customs officer as she handed over her passport to be stamped. She was feeling good. All her meetings had gone extremely well, the black-tie reception had been great fun, and she'd taken a day at either end of her assignment to wander the museums and art galleries of Santiago. Still, she'd be glad to be home. She always was.

She had lots of time to get a cab from Kennedy to LaGuardia for her Toronto flight. But as she waited patiently for her bags to be checked, she was smiling for quite another reason. Now that she was on her way home, she realized she'd cured herself of Jared Holt.

At first she'd carried him with her everywhere; even in the eddying crowds of Santiago she had unconsciously singled out all the tall, dark-haired men, and her heart had automatically speeded up. But somehow as the days had passed in a foreign country, speaking another language, she'd managed to distance herself from him, and to thank her lucky stars she'd escaped when she had. She had more than that to be thankful for. She'd also been—inadvertently—protected against pregnancy.

Seven months ago she'd met a man called Peter Damien in Bangkok; she'd liked him very much. While the head office of his pharmaceutical company was based in London, he had made occasional trips to Toronto. They'd dated several times. Almost certain she wanted an affair with him, Devon had planned to meet him in London. She'd visited a gynecologist there, and, because in her early twenties she'd had problems with the pill, had had an IUD inserted.

Then she'd discovered from an associate that Peter had been engaged to a woman in Sydney, Australia, for the last ten months. She'd been deeply upset, not so much by Peter's perfidy, although that had been bad enough, as by its unnerving recall of her longtime affair with Steve all those years ago.

Steve Danford. Cultured, good-looking, a cardiologist with an international health agency. Devon had fallen in love with him at the age of twenty-two, had had a long distance affair with him for three years—and quite by chance had found out he'd been married for the last eight years. She'd been devastated.

Men weren't to be trusted. That was his legacy. A legacy her mother's multiple marriages had done nothing to assuage and that Peter had reactivated. But—and this was where Devon was truly grateful—the night she'd spent with Jared she'd still been safeguarded against pregnancy. The last thing on her mind when Jared had, literally, swept her off her feet had been birth control. She now understood how women had unplanned pregnancies. She might have had one herself if it hadn't been for Peter.

Politely Devon answered the customs officer's rote questions, watched him stamp her documents, and then walked through the frosted glass doors into the waiting area, where she edged around the crowd toward the taxi signs. A tall, black-haired man moved to intercept her. "Hello, Devon," he said.

Devon almost dropped her laptop computer. Gaping upward, she said foolishly, "J-Jared," and not for anything could she have masked the joy that whirled through her body in all the colors of the rainbow.

His lashes flickered. "Come along, we haven't got much time."

Cured? Talk about self-deception, she thought, and stammered, "I—I beg your pardon?"

"We haven't got much time. The concert starts at eight. By any chance have you got a decent dress in that bag?"

"Concert?" she repeated blankly.

"Yo-Yo Ma."

Trying desperately to gather her wits, swept by a host of memories, not one of which was suitable for a busy airport, Devon said the first thing that came to mind. "I couldn't get a ticket."

"Are you okay?"

It was exactly the same question he'd asked her after their first, tumultuous lovemaking. Hot color crept up her cheeks. "It's just—I wasn't expecting to see you," she said in magnificent understatement. Come on, Devon, pull yourself together. Do you have to make it so glaringly obvious that the sight of him has bowled you over? Cool it!

"The limo's waiting for us," he said, and took her suitcase from her unresisting fingers.

Devon planted her feet and said, "Hold on, I'm missing something here. I'm on my way to Toronto, Jared. My flight leaves in a couple of hours."

"I've rebooked you. You're leaving on the first flight in the morning."

"You can't have," she squawked. "I've got my ticket right here in my purse."

"I play squash with the president of the company."

His smile was perfunctory, his shoulders every bit as broad as she remembered them, and clearly he was expecting her to fall flat at his feet in gratitude. "You can't go rearranging my life like that!"

"I already have. Two of the Bach cello suites are on the program."

"Bribery," she snorted.

"Persuasion."

"How did you know I was landing in New York?"

"Your mother."

"I'll throttle her!"

"Have you got a dress?"

"Not the turquoise one," Devon said in outright defiance.

"Just as well, wouldn't you say?" Jared answered smoothly.

"Let me get this straight. You—along with the president of the airline—have canceled my flight out of LaGuardia." Jared nodded. "Without even asking my permission."

"You were in Chile," Jared said with a crooked grin.

"Jared, I am never going to bed with you again," Devon announced loudly. To her mortification, a couple of passengers turned their heads, staring at her.

"I haven't asked you to. The limo's this way."

And Devon, fighting the twin urges to hit Jared over the head with her computer and to burst out laughing, found herself trotting beside him through the crowds.

CHAPTER SIX

THE limo had a chauffeur named Hubert; the limo belonged to Jared. Well, of course, thought Devon. Jared's rolling in money. What's a limo here or there? She was only surprised he didn't own the whole darned airline.

She thanked Hubert for taking her bags and with outward composure slid into her seat. Her pantsuit was both elegant and uncrushable, and she'd brushed her hair smooth and replenished her make-up before they'd landed. For all of which she was extremely grateful. Now all she had to do was enjoy a concert she'd longed to attend, and stay out of Jared's bed.

No problem. She might not be cured of him to quite the extent she'd thought, but she did have a policy of never making the same mistake twice.

He was sitting at least a foot from her in the back seat and showed no signs of wanting to close the gap. He hadn't even tried to kiss her at the airport. Maybe the shoe was on the other foot and he was cured of her. In which case, she wasn't in the slightest danger. Not if he no longer wanted to go to bed with her. Devon's lips compressed. Then she heard him say, "I've laid on a light snack at my place...I made a reservation for dinner after the concert. Hubert will drive you to LaGuardia in the morning."

"From my hotel."

"My penthouse has a guest suite."

She said coolly, "How nice for you."

"Don't be bitchy, Devon. It's not your style."

"How would you know?"

"Oh, I know a lot about you," he said softly, his eyes

wandering the length of her body in its forest green suit. "Except for one thing. Why did you leave in the middle of the night?"

"Are you sure you want the answer?"

"I asked."

Assailed by a blast of horns from the traffic tie-up on the other side of the street, Devon said deliberately, "I was ashamed of what I'd done. I felt cheap, as though I'd betrayed all my principles."

"How very high-minded of you."

"How very old-fashioned of me," she responded tightly. "I've never done that before—climbed in the sack with a man I'd scarcely met."

"So what's so special about me?"

She'd walked right into that one, and had no intentions of answering him. "You said at the time that we had one night. No tomorrow. Why the postmortem, Jared?"

"I don't like loose ends."

"Hardly a flattering description of me."

"I hate flattery. Don't you?"

They were fencing with each other, thought Devon, and felt vibrantly alert, as if she were fighting for her life. Even though he was wearing a tailored business suit, Jared looked as dangerous as any musketeer. She'd crossed him. She'd left "The Oaks" before he'd given her permission to leave. She said coolly, "Is there a lock on the guest suite door?"

"There is. And an antique desk you can pull across it."

"Cat and mouse, Jared...you sure like to play games."

For the first time he laughed. "You're no mouse, Devon Fraser."

"Just as you're no tabby cat. A mountain lion, more likely."

"You flatter me."

Suddenly breathless, Devon muttered, "I never dish out flattery and I hope that desk's heavy."

"Solid oak."

She loved crossing swords with him; for if she felt alert, she also felt fully alive. Yet she knew in a flash of intuition that the blades were sharp, and any duel with Jared could be lethal. "You're not used to women who act on their own initiative."

"You make a pleasant change."

"A diversion," she said with a touch of bitterness. "I had an affair once with a man who thought of me as a diversion. And a while ago I nearly did it again. Silly me. Don't you do that to me, Jared."

He shifted restlessly in his seat. "The traffic's heavier than I'd expected."

All Devon's vitality drained away. She got the message: for Jared she was a diversion. A woman interestingly different, amusing, and easily discarded. History repeating itself. The concert had better be good, she thought, leaned back in her seat and shut her eyes, closing him out.

The limo gathered momentum, then stopped and started at a series of lights. Wishing she could doze off, Devon eventually felt Jared squeeze her elbow. He said formally, "We're here."

Moments later she was entering the foyer of an elegant stone building overlooking Central Park. Jared had the whole top floor; the guest suite did indeed have a key and the desk looked immovable.

"Why don't we eat first?" Jared said easily. "Out on the roof garden, whenever you're ready."

The door shut behind him. Devon put down her computer and looked around.

The room had spare, clean lines, the colors were vibrant, the floor a gleaming expanse of parquet, and the furniture an eclectic mixture of antique and modern. The bedroom, all cool blues and whites, charmed her in its simplicity, while the bathroom was total luxury. Swiftly she hung up her dress, replenished her lipstick, and left the suite.

Whether Jared had any intention of seducing her made no difference. She was going to stay in control of the evening. She. Not he.

The roof garden, bounded by an ivy-covered brick wall, had blue and cream hydrangeas in glazed Chinese pots, and was shaded by cedars and weeping birch trees: an oasis of privacy in the very heart of the city. Smoked pheasant, pasta salad and fresh brioches were laid out on a spotless linen cloth. Jared had stripped off his jacket and tie. Averting her eyes from the tangle of dark hair at his throat, Devon began to eat with frank enjoyment, the distant roar of the traffic oddly soothing. As casually as if he were a chance acquaintance, she described some of her experiences in Chile, and was fascinated by the intelligence of his questions, the speed with which he could reach conclusions. Then, all too soon, it was time to get dressed.

Devon showered quickly, leaving her hair loose on her shoulders. Her dress, rose-pink, was artfully simple, long-sleeved, hugging her breasts then falling in graceful folds to the floor. A quartz necklace shimmered against her skin. Her shawl was cream, of finely woven wool with a silk fringe.

She looked like the heroine of a Jane Austen novel, she thought wryly, and not at all like the sexy maid-of-honor at her mother's wedding. This dress wouldn't get her into any trouble.

But what Devon didn't see was the way the dress clung softly to her body as she moved, nor the glow of excitement in her cheeks as she left her suite. Jared was waiting for her, formidably attractive in a tuxedo. He said flatly, "Ready?"

She should be pleased he hadn't complimented her on

her appearance, Devon thought, as they drove the short distance to Carnegie Hall, the blare of taxi horns accompanying them the whole way, the sidewalks a jostle of pedestrians. But she wasn't pleased. She hated being treated like a maiden aunt. Or like Aunt Bessie. And how was that for inconsistency?

Jared had the best seats in the house. Trying to look blasé about this, Devon sat down and buried her nose in the program. Then the lights dimmed slowly. Unable to help herself, Devon gave Jared a childlike grin of pure anticipation and turned her full attention to the stage.

Just over two hours later, the concert ended; Devon, however, couldn't have said how long it had lasted. Transported, she got up after the encore and the storm of applause, scarcely aware of Jared offering her his arm, or of their slow progress out to the street. She always needed to be quiet after any kind of music that had deeply moved her, whether Bach or *Les Miserables*, and was grateful to him for respecting this.

In the restaurant, which was just around the corner, the maître d' knew Jared, and their table was secluded. For Devon, the music had done away with anything petty or small-minded; in the soft flicker of candlelight, she leaned toward her companion and said, "Jared, thank you. That was—well, I can't find any words. Just thank you."

He looked at her broodingly. "You mean it, don't you?"

"Of course I do—you think I'd tell you anything but the truth after that glorious music?"

As if the words were wrenched from him, he said, "You keep taking me by surprise, Devon...I never know how you're going to react."

"Why don't you try taking me as I am?" she said impulsively. "What you see is what you get."

"You think it's coincidence I date an actress? What you see isn't what you get. Lise is open about it, that's all."

Devon said steadily, "But it was me you took to the concert."

"Yeah..." He detached her fingers from the leather menu, staring at them as if they could tell him something. Then, abruptly, he put them down. "Let's order."

"Jared, did a woman hurt you when you were young?" Devon hadn't meant to ask that. Her heart beating uncomfortably fast, she waited for his reply.

His jaw clenched. "I recommend the brandied duck."

She didn't want to quarrel with him, and was somehow sure she had her answer. When the waiter reappeared, she gave her order and switched to other, safer topics, again discovering him to be a witty and knowledgeable conversationalist who brought out the best in herself. They drank a bottle of full-bodied Bordeaux with the duck, after which Devon ate a concoction of Viennese chocolate and heavy cream with enormous pleasure. Looking up, she found Jared watching her; brooding again, she thought with a shiver of unease, his midnight-blue eyes inscrutable. Dabbing her lips with her napkin, she said abruptly, "We should go...I have to be up early tomorrow. Unless you want coffee?"

"No. I'm ready to leave." He signaled for the bill, dealt with it swiftly, and got up.

Not to her surprise, Hubert was waiting outside the restaurant; they drove home in complete silence. She'd eaten too much, Devon thought moodily. And one thing was certain. She wouldn't need to shift the desk. Jared had scarcely touched her the whole evening, and had made absolutely no move to kiss her.

In the elevator she stared absorbedly at the control panel. Jared unlocked the door to his apartment, waiting for her to precede him. As he bolted the door, she turned to him and said politely, "That was a lovely meal, Jared, thank you. Now I'm—"

He pulled her to him, running his fingers over her face like a blind man who needed reassurance that she was real. Then he kissed her softly parted lips with the fierceness of a predator.

In a swirl of relief and sheer pleasure, Devon knew this was what she'd been longing for all evening. She then stopped thinking altogether as she kissed him back, clasping the hard bone of his jawline in her hands, running her fingers over his ears, into his thick, dark hair. His mouth left hers to slide down her throat and bury itself in her cleavage; her nipples hardened, her body bonelessly surrendering itself to him.

Afterward, she had very little recollection of how they'd got from the hall to his bedroom. She did remember the first sight of him naked, his lean, muscular body both utterly familiar to her and powerfully, dauntingly other. And she remembered him muttering against her breast, "You are protected, are you, Devon? Last time I didn't even think to ask."

"Yes, of course...oh, Jared, do that again. Again...please."

"So you like what I'm doing? Tell me you like it, Devon."

"Yes, yes, I love it, can't you tell?" she whimpered, and opened to him as a rose to the sunlight.

They made love the night through, as though neither of them could get enough of the other; in brief interludes they slept, awakening each time to the heat and hunger of flesh on flesh. At dawn, exhausted, Devon fell asleep in Jared's arms, and woke to the jarring voice of a radio announcer. Her eyes flew open.

Jared was leaning over her on one elbow, watching her. She smiled at him drowsily. "It can't be morning...not already."

He didn't smile back. The grey light sifted through the

curtains, shadowing the angles of his collarbone, the implacable line of his shoulders. His eyes, those night-sky eyes, were unreadable. Smothering a quick unease, Devon added, "What time is it?"

"You'd better get up. Hubert will be outside in half an hour."

He looked like a stranger, cold and distant. Devon pushed herself up against the pillows. "Jared, what's wrong?"

"This time you didn't leave in the middle of the night."

An ice-cold knife slid between her ribs. "I don't understand...what are you getting at?"

"This time was on my terms. You in my bed for as long as I wanted you here." His deep baritone roughened. "How dare you leave 'The Oaks' without as much as saying goodbye?"

The point of the knife had found her heart. In an appalled whisper, Devon said, "All our love-making last night—you were out for revenge?"

"Lovemaking? We don't love each other, Devon," he snarled. "So don't dress up what we do in bed with sloppy, romantic claptrap."

With an incoherent cry of distress, she pulled away from him. "The concert, the dinner, the whole evening was a set-up?"

"I wanted you here. In my bed. And that's what I got."

"On your terms," Devon repeated numbly. She felt as though she was bleeding to death internally, as though the wound he'd dealt her was mortal. For a crazy moment she wondered if she was dreaming, a nightmare from which she'd waken to find herself sheltered in Jared's embrace. And then she took another look at his hostile gaze and knew this was real.

He'd tricked her. He'd taken her to bed out of anger. And then she remembered something else. In a faraway voice she scarcely recognized as her own, she said, "Is this what you call taming me, Jared?"

A muscle twitched in his jaw. "You'd better hurry—you wouldn't want to miss your plane."

Pain had coalesced along every nerve in Devon's body; her eyes burned with unshed tears. Determined not to cry in front of him, she took refuge in an anger to match his own. "Of course not—I'd hate for you to have to bother the president of the airline again. What a manipulator you are, Jared! Cold-blooded, throwing your position and your money around to get whatever you want...I hate your guts. And I despise myself for having been taken in by you. For spending any time in your bed. On anyone's terms."

In a lithe movement she got to her feet, fiercely unashamed of her nakedness. "I'll never do it again. Never!"

"All I'd have to do is kiss you, and you'd do it again."

"So is that how you get your kicks—making love with women who loathe you?"

He surged to his feet. "I don't believe in love!" he blazed. "Love makes the world go round? Don't make me laugh! Do you know what love is, Devon? It's commerce, it's cold, hard cash. It propels an industry of flowers and perfumes and romantic retreats—just ask me; I own some of them and they make me big bucks. But it's all based on a myth. Lust is what brought us together—for God's sake, quit dressing it up as anything else!"

Too angry to bother guarding her tongue, Devon flared, "Just to set the record straight, I'm not—repeat not—even the slightest bit in love with you. For which I'm practically down on my knees with gratitude. But when I get into bed with a man, I expect to be treated with some consideration. As a woman with feelings. Not like some kind of Barbie doll. Or a chunk of stock you can buy or sell according to your whim."

"When I take a woman," Jared rasped, "I damn well do it the way I want to."

"Then you're not a rich man at all," Devon said with icy clarity.

His jaw tightened. For a split second she was sure she saw raw agony flicker across his face, as though she'd struck him. But before she could even consider responding to it, his face had closed against her into a contemptuous mask. "You don't have a clue in hell what you're talking about," he said.

"Yes, I do—you just don't want to admit I might be right." In spite of herself, the words burst out, each one seared with pain. "How could you kiss me, caress me...when all you wanted was revenge? That's a terrible thing to do! How *could* you, Jared?"

"It was easy," he said.

Devon said bitterly, "It was me that was easy. All I cost you was a concert ticket and a fancy dinner. I hope you got a bargain, Jared—I hope you got value for money. It's just too bad you're not getting a repeat, isn't it?"

"Maybe I don't want a repeat."

Why would he? she thought. He'd proved his point. Suddenly Devon had had enough. Exhaustion washed over her and her anger vanished. Perilously close to tears, holding her voice steady with an effort, she said, "You know what I hate the most? That I was so gullible. Don't bother getting dressed; I'll see myself out." Not even deigning to see if any of her clothes were lying on the bedroom floor, she walked out of the room and closed the door behind her.

You're not a rich man at all...

Jared stood very still. It wasn't true. Of course it wasn't. He had more money than he knew what to do with, along with all the power that money brought; his business empire, moreover, was endlessly interesting to him. And he could have any woman he wanted, when he wanted her.

Including Devon.

He'd wanted Devon. She'd spent the night in his bed, and this time she'd left when he'd been ready for her to leave. What more did he want than that?

How stricken she'd looked when he'd finally gotten through to her that it had all been for revenge. Stricken. Devastated. As hurt as though he'd stuck a knife between her ribs and twisted the blade.

That had been his aim, hadn't it? To hurt Devon, as he'd been hurt when he'd woken at "The Oaks" to an empty bed.

Through the closed door, he heard her unbolt the door into the lobby. He could have pulled on his trousers and gone after her. Stopped her from leaving. He didn't. Like a statue, Jared stood by the bed, remembering how generously she'd given herself to him, her throaty laughter, her frantic breathing and broken cries in the moments of climax.

Lust. Sex. Dammit, there was nothing wrong with either one. But he and Devon hadn't made love. To make love, Jared thought viciously, you had to know something about love. To be in love. He'd never once fallen in love in all his thirty-eight years. As for why he hadn't, any Manhattan shrink—for an exorbitant sum of money—could have told him he was angry because his mother had died when he was only five, abandoning him, and that he'd lost all trust in women after Beatrice had dazzled his bereaved father into a hasty marriage. Beatrice. How he'd hated her.

Add to that years of being chased by everything in skirts because he was filthy rich, and you had a man immune to that charming fallacy called love.

He didn't need a shrink. He didn't need Devon, no matter what the expression on her face. He certainly didn't need to fall in love. What he did need was to bring his mind round to the currency collapse in the Far East.

Business as usual.

It was one of his unbreakable rules never to allow a woman to come between him and the world of business. Devon Fraser wasn't about to become the exception to that rule.

Five weeks later, Devon flew in from Australia. She'd spent a very productive month in Sydney and Papua New Guinea, and her apartment had never looked so good.

She'd picked up some kind of tropical bug while she was away. In Papua New Guinea, probably, even though she'd followed all her usual meticulous precautions. She felt, to put it mildly, like death warmed over. The first thing she did, even before unpacking, was phone her physician to make an appointment. Luckily she hit on a cancellation; she could get in late that afternoon.

Unpack. Shower. Pick up a few groceries, buy flowers for her living room. Ordinarily Devon loved the routine of settling back into her condo. And this time she was home for a while; once she'd written up her report, she had three weeks of well-earned vacation.

But as she opened her almost empty refrigerator, a pen and piece of paper in her hand, nausea cramped in her belly. She ran for the bathroom, and for the second time that day upchucked into the toilet. Last time had been on the jumbo jet. The washrooms of jet planes weren't designed for women with upset stomachs.

Afterward, Devon washed her face in cold water, looking at herself dispassionately in the mirror over the sink. There were dark shadows under her eyes, and her skin looked bleached. She didn't remotely resemble the glowing creature who'd gone to a concert in New York with a man who'd attracted her as a moth to the flame.

Maybe Jared was the reason she felt so lousy. Nothing to do with a tropical virus. Try as she might, this time she hadn't been able to rid herself of his presence. He haunted her, awake and asleep. Her body craved his touch even as her spirit felt flayed by his cruelty.

The worst part of the whole situation was how atrociously her radar had been off. She'd mistaken his passion, the undoubted tenderness he'd shown her in bed, for caring. But it hadn't been caring at all. It had been vengeance. A crude assertion of his will, and she of no more value to him than a stash of bills.

Less, probably, she thought, with a touch of his own cynicism.

She'd misjudged Steve and Peter. And now Jared.

Pretty stupid of her. How could she be so smart when it came to the intricacies of mining laws and so dumb around half the human race?

But at least she wasn't in love with him. She knew that for a fact. Obsessed with him, yes. But not in love.

Obsession. What a horrible word.

Devon went back into the kitchen and grimly started her grocery list. Once she got back into a routine and caught up on her sleep, she'd feel fine. With luck she'd be back from the doctor by five-thirty. Then the evening was her own, to do with as she pleased. She'd turn on the TV and veg out, and go to bed really early.

What she wouldn't do was think about Jared.

As it happened, the doctor had had another cancellation and Devon was home by quarter past five. In her cool airy living room, where the pot of scarlet cyclamen that she'd bought that morning flared against the reflections of the sun, she sat down hard on the chesterfield and stared at the ivory-painted wall.

She didn't have a tropical bug. She was pregnant.

Seven weeks pregnant.

The father, of course, was Jared. She must have conceived the first night they'd made love, at "The Oaks."

Her IUD was no longer in place, so the doctor had informed her, and it was then that she'd recollected the dreadful menstrual cramps she'd had in Borneo four months ago. That, she was now convinced, was when it had dislodged itself. She'd been too caught up in some very difficult negotiations to pay much attention to her body. Nor had birth control been her top priority.

Pregnant. With Jared's child. It couldn't be true! What in heaven's name was she going to do?

Devon got up. She paced back and forth. She did a load of wash, tried to eat some pasta and lost it an hour later in the bathroom. And the whole time her thoughts chased each other round her brain like hamsters in a cage.

Marriage wasn't even an option. She hated Jared and he despised her. He'd betrayed her in New York, defiled her very being when he'd treated her body with such passionate desire and her soul like a piece of dirt. How could she ever trust him again? No, she couldn't possibly marry Jared.

Yet everything in her cried out against abortion. In the early days at her job, when she'd been based in Ottawa, her friend Judy had had an abortion, and had then regretted what she'd done; Devon could remember the floods of tears, the long months of depression that had followed. Besides, despite her own appalling situation, she already felt ferociously protective of her unborn child: a bone-deep reaction that had taken her by surprise. Was this what was meant by the mothering instinct? She didn't know. But she was sure that, for her, abortion would violate her conscience in much the same way that Jared's revenge had violated her soul.

But if she had the baby, she couldn't keep it a secret. Jared would know whose it was, just from the timing. If

the child resembled its father, which was all too likely, so
would her mother and Benson. Perhaps she could give the
baby up for adoption? But how could she hide a pregnancy
from Alicia for seven more months? She'd be bound to see
her mother and Benson during that time.

Then, with a nasty jolt, Devon suddenly realized the obvious. She was carrying the grandchild Alicia and Benson
had been waiting for: one more strand in the noose so inexorably tightening around her. How could she tell her
mother and stepfather she was giving up their grandchild
for adoption?

There was no way out. No way at all.

She was nothing like a hamster in a cage. She was like
a wolf in a steel leg snare. Trapped, and knowing itself
trapped. Desperate only for escape.

The telephone rang. Convinced it must be Jared, Devon
stared at the phone in horror, let it ring four times and then
reluctantly picked it up. "Hello?" she mumbled.

"Darling? Is that you?"

"Hello, Mother."

"When did you get home?"

"This morning."

"Darling, you sound awful...did I wake you?"

Devon made a valiant effort to put some energy in her
voice. "I picked up some kind of bug while I was away,"
she lied. "I'm not feeling the greatest."

Alicia went on at some length about Devon's job and all
the reasons why she should quit it. Then she said, "We're
having a birthday dinner for Benson next week; you'll be
better by then, darling, won't you? I thought we'd have it
in the city just so you'll be sure to be there. I don't think
Jared can make it, he's down south somewhere, so I'm
depending on you. Although Patrick—remember him?—
he'll be in town."

Face Alicia and Benson next week, knowing she was

carrying Jared's child? Out of the question. "I don't know, Mother, I'll have to see how I'm feeling."

"You've got to come, Devon. It's so important to me that my family and Benson's grow together, spend more time with each other...I'm so happy, darling, it's frightening."

Devon suppressed a quiver of laughter that could all too easily turn into hysteria. The family already was growing together. Right here in her own body. "I'll see how I feel," she temporized. "You could always bring the photos from your honeymoon."

As she'd thought, this set Alicia off on a string of reminiscences. Five minutes later Devon put down the receiver, still without committing herself to the dinner.

The living room wall was as blank of solutions as it had been all evening. She couldn't avoid her mother indefinitely. Get it over with, Devon. Take the bull by the horns, jump in the deep end, just do it. Go to the dinner. After all, it was too soon for the baby to show.

And Jared wouldn't be there.

CHAPTER SEVEN

THE following week, Jared flew home two days early from the Exumas, where he'd been inspecting the completion of a new luxury resort. Stripping off his tie, wishing New York wasn't as hot as the Caribbean with none of its charm, he checked the messages on his machine. Lise, of course. She was in Toronto doing a one-woman show for a couple of weeks. The other message was from Alicia.

No messages from Devon. No reason why Devon would phone him and every reason why she wouldn't. Quickly he dialed "The Oaks."

Alicia always sounded as if she was face to face with a starving grizzly when she was talking to him, he thought impatiently. Then his attention sharpened. "...a dinner party for your father's birthday. In Toronto on Friday, at Verdi's. Could you come, Jared? I hadn't expected you to be back in time, and I'd love to have the family all together."

Yeah, he thought, one big happy family, and with brutal force subdued the memory of Devon's tangled blond hair on his pillow. If he went to Toronto, he'd see her again. And would that rid him of this never-ending compulsion to be with her? Breathing in the perfume of her skin, watching laughter lift the corners of her delectable mouth? Enjoying her swift intelligence, her warm contralto voice? He hadn't even been able to swim at the resort's private beach without thinking about the mysterious depths of her sea-blue eyes.

Or the pain in them when he'd told her why he'd taken her to bed that night in the penthouse.

"What time?" he rapped.

"Seven-thirty. Devon's coming with Patrick; isn't it nice that he's in town?"

Subduing a murderous flare of jealousy, Jared said smoothly, "Would it be all right if I brought Lise? She's also in Toronto, as it happens."

"Of course," Alicia said. "The more the merrier."

After a further exchange of meaningless pleasantries, Jared rang off. Merriment wasn't high on his list. Not if Devon was going to the dinner with Patrick. Did that mean she was dating him? It probably did. Devon had liked Patrick from the start. And why not? They had a lot in common, and his cousin was a decent guy who—Jared would be willing to bet—had never in his life taken a woman to bed to teach her a lesson.

The lesson had sure as hell rebounded. He'd made a major miscalculation in assuming that if he took Devon to bed on his terms in New York, he'd be done with her.

Done with her? That was the laugh of the century.

Jared and Lise were five minutes early arriving at Verdi's, a trendy restaurant with an excellent small band and a much-touted Italian cuisine. Lise looked stunning in a dove-gray suit with a plunging neckline; she was clinging to his arm in a way that already made him regret inviting her. He wasn't worried about her feelings; it had taken him only one or two dates with Lise to realize her emotional life was reserved for the stage and her ambitions were two-fold: to get to the top of her profession and to marry a rich man. No, Lise could look after herself. The problem was his own fierce impatience to see Devon again, and the need to conceal that impatience from everyone else.

Devon and Patrick were ten minutes late, minutes that felt like an eternity to Jared. He was making small talk—very small talk—with Alicia when he had his first glimpse of Devon in well over a month. She was wearing a teal-blue tunic lavish with gold embroidery over the briefest of teal-blue skirts; her legs seemed to go on forever. Her hair was a mass of curls and her make-up dramatic. Her slender ankles, the sway of her hips, even the carriage of her head, filled him with a chaotic mixture of hunger, rage and pain.

Just as she left the foyer, one of the waiters, a young man with carrot-red hair, passed near her. She stopped him, briefly resting a hand on his arm. The young man's face lit up. They exchanged a few animated words, wide smiles, and then the waiter kept on his way. As Patrick said something to Devon, Alicia glanced up at Jared and said gloomily, "Another of Devon's lame ducks."

"What do you mean?" he said sharply.

"She worked at a hangout for street kids for a couple of years. Before that she used to stay overnight at a battered women's shelter." Alicia gave a delicate shudder. "It used to worry me to death. And I'm always so afraid when she's overseas she'll interfere in something she shouldn't. She can't stand to see anything mistreated...whether it's a chicken or a child."

Devon's not after my money. She never was.

Jared's jaw dropped. For a moment, so clear were the words in his head, he was convinced he'd said them out loud. But Alicia was still gazing at her daughter, and no one else was paying him any attention. Feeling as though he'd been hit on the head with a two by four, he watched Devon weave her way through the tables. Benson stood up to greet her. Automatically, Jared did the same.

From a distance she'd looked as brilliant as a butterfly. Close up, she looked godawful, Jared thought; shadows under her eyes that no amount of make-up could disguise, her skin so pale it was translucent. She kissed her mother on the cheek, hugged Benson and greeted Aunt Bessie, Uncle Leonard and Lise with a polished social ease. Then she turned to him. "Good evening, Jared," she said with as much feeling as if he were a cardboard cutout.

"Are you ill?" he demanded.

Her chin tilted. "I picked up a tropical bug of some kind in Papua New Guinea. I'm fine."

"You don't look fine."

"I already have a mother," she seethed. "I don't need another one."

He pulled out the chair next to him, the chair he'd made sure would be empty. "Sit down before you fall down."

Her eyes flickered round the table. Patrick had already claimed the seat next to Lise. "Still at your little games?" Devon snapped, and sat down.

Jared didn't answer. His previous emotions had changed into something far more complex. Concern? Anxiety? Outright fear? She looked brittle, he thought, as though she could snap if someone said a wrong word to her. Her fingers were restlessly toying with the cutlery; one of the things—one of the many things—he'd noticed about her, had been how quietly she could sit. He'd found it oddly restful.

He said flatly, "What's wrong, Devon?"

"I've told you what's wrong." She gave the waiter the smile she hadn't given Jared. "I'll have a Perrier with lime, please."

"Glenfiddich, straight up," Jared said shortly. "How did you know the other waiter, the one with the red hair?"

For the first time, Devon looked straight at him. Her eyes, normally so expressive, were blank, totally remote, and this frightened Jared more than her pallor and her air of fragility. "That's none of your business," she said in a voice too low for anyone else to hear. "I thought you weren't coming tonight, or I wouldn't have come myself. You treated me like dirt in New York—like a toy you were tired of, so you smashed it. I have nothing more to say to you. Nothing.''

"What kind of bug? Have you been to a specialist?''

Her fingers clenched around her knife. As though, he thought humorlessly, she'd like to stick it in him and watch him bleed to death. Slowly. All over the carpet. He added, ''I've done a lot of travel in the tropics...you've got to be so careful.''

Careful, Devon thought. Right on, Jared. If she'd been more careful, paid more attention to her own body, she wouldn't be in the mess she was in. Trying to inject some energy in her voice, she said, ''Keep your advice for some-one who gives a damn.''

His intuition, for which he was famous because it had guided him so often and so successfully through the shoals of the stock market and the corporate jungle, was now yell-ing at him that Devon's troubles weren't just some tropical bug, bad though that could be. No, there was more going on. Unfortunately, his same intuition was batting zero when it came to defining what that could be. He didn't have a clue.

And why did he feel as though he wanted to protect her? Comfort her? Do anything within his power to relieve the lines of strain around her mouth, to make her laugh? He'd never felt this way about a woman. The first sign of deep emotional waters and he was gone. Out of there.

Before Jared could think of anything to say—and he was rarely at a loss for words—Devon started talking to Aunt Bessie's husband, Uncle Leonard, who was sitting across from her. Moodily Jared drank his whisky and picked up the menu, which was as heavy as a piece of slab board. The waiter returned. Devon ordered a small salad and the mildest of pastas. She hadn't even touched her Perrier.

Alicia, who was at the head of the table, on his other side, bravely tried to engage him in conversation. Maybe, he thought, Alicia hadn't been after Benson's money any more than Devon had been after his. From the little he'd seen of them, Benson and Alicia seemed genuinely affectionate and very happy together.

You might be a whiz kid at the stock market. But you're way off base on the personal stuff.

This thought, too, had come out of left field. It was his night for insights, he thought sardonically. Until he'd met Devon, when had he ever needed any expertise with women's feelings? He'd always been the one in control. Keeping any emotion firmly under wraps, where it belonged.

"...do you think, Jared?"

"Sorry, Alicia, what did you say?" he stumbled, and tried to pay attention.

The first course arrived. Devon picked at her salad, keeping her eyes on her plate. Jared drank his Mantua squash soup and said, in an effort to get some kind of response from her, "I brought your dress with me, Devon." He'd also brought everything else she'd been wearing the night of the concert, her lacy pale pink underwear and her wisps of stockings.

Devon winced. Remembering how she'd abandoned the dress on his bedroom floor when she'd so precipitately left the penthouse, she watched a piece of zucchini fall from her fork. She'd never been fond of zucchini. Especially raw. She suddenly pushed away from the table, gasped, "Excuse me," and fled for the washroom.

Jared half got up, then sank back in his chair. He said urgently, "Alicia, I'm worried about her."

"Me, too," said Alicia. "But she hates it when I fuss. So I try very hard not to."

"I'll ask her to dance when she comes back. Maybe I can find out what's wrong."

Alicia said with genuine gratitude, "That's very kind of you, Jared."

Feeling thoroughly ashamed of himself, for he'd been far from kind to Alicia in the past and he wasn't at all sure that his motives toward Devon were anything to do with kindness, Jared asked Uncle Leonard about his varicose veins. His uncle loved to talk about his ailments, a tendency which drove Aunt Bessie to distraction. As he listened with one ear to all the gory details of the last operation, Jared was keeping his eye out for Devon.

When he saw her appear at the far end of the room, he left the table and went to meet her.

Devon watched him threading his way through the tables toward her, a tall, commanding figure who moved with the economy of a predator. She'd had warning from Patrick, when he'd picked her up, that Jared was coming tonight. So at least she hadn't had to face him unawares. Wishing she were anywhere on earth but at Verdi's, Devon tilted her chin and waited for Jared. No point in trying to avoid him; she knew better than that.

He said easily, "Let's dance, Devon."

At least on the dance floor she wouldn't have to look at everyone else's food. Morning sickness, she thought unhappily, was a misnomer. All-day-and-well-into-the-evening sickness would be more accurate. At the edge of the dance floor, she turned to Jared, gazing at the tiny seahorses on his silk tie.

Pierced by compassion, Jared said huskily, "Devon, won't you tell me what's the matter?"

Briefly she closed her eyes. "No."

She hadn't denied there was something bothering her. She was merely refusing to tell him what it was. And how could he blame her? His actions toward her that morning in New York were beginning to seem considerably below the usual high standards he expected of himself. Wishing she didn't look so goddamned breakable, Jared took her into his arms, and was instantly and treacherously besieged by memory. Her height, her perfume, the gentle concavity of her waist, all so well known to him. So strongly desired.

He said choppily, "There's something I need to say to you."

She was looking past his shoulder, and again he had that sense of her utter remoteness. Then, as his brain made a sudden horrified leap, he stumbled over his own feet. "Are you just fobbing everyone off? Have you got something really serious—like cancer?"

"No," she repeated in the same toneless voice.

His heart was still pounding as though he'd been running. He swallowed, aware of a flood of relief, aware, too, that she wasn't lying to him. He was almost sure she never lied. The truth, for Devon, would be the shortest and least complicated distance between two points. He said, "I got dysentery once after a stint in India. No fun."

Devon didn't bother replying. She was holding herself rigidly, dancing with mechanical aptitude and none of her usual grace. Jared said evenly, "When your mother told me about how you used to work with street kids and battered women—it hit me like a ton of bricks. You've never been after my money, Devon. I know that now…I'm only sorry I said so."

"My mother talks too much," Devon said expressionlessly.

Had he, subconsciously, figured that once he apologized, Devon would melt into his arms? He'd never apologized to a woman in his life. How would he know what came next? But if he'd anticipated an instant reconciliation, he couldn't have been more wrong. Devon was still dancing like a plastic doll; like the Barbie doll she'd once mentioned, he thought, and said stiffly, "I misjudged you. I apologize."

Her lashes dropped to hide her eyes. "Fine," she said.

"I can stay in town until tomorrow night. Have lunch with me, Devon."

"I don't want to."

"Will you for Pete's sake look at me?"

She stopped dead. "I've said no, Jared. That little word you have such difficulty with... I shouldn't have come tonight, it was stupid of me. Now will you please take me back to our table?"

He could start a blazing row with her in the middle of the dance floor. He could throw her across his shoulder and abduct her, a course of action that appealed to him a great deal. Jared said tersely, "So you hold grudges."

"Jared," Devon said, "you and I slept together in New York. You made love to me the whole night through, and then told me it was all a set-up, a power play to teach me who was the boss. Give me one good reason why I should trust anything you say or do. Ever again."

The muscles knotted between his shoulders, Jared steered her round two other couples. According to Devon—and it wasn't the first time she'd said this—he'd made love to her that night. Made *love*? Oh, no, he thought, he hadn't made love. He'd bedded her. Making love wasn't on his agenda. Never had been.

She said coldly, still gazing at his tie, "You apologized just now with as much feeling in your voice as if you were ordering a salad from the waiter. Why should I believe you? It's probably step one in whatever campaign you're waging next. Because you hate to lose, don't you? You can't stand to have a woman who's not falling all over you." Suddenly her shoulders slumped, and she swayed on her feet, her cheeks paper-white. "Don't you understand?" she cried. "You manipulated me like a piece of ticker tape, Jared! Cheapened me. And yourself, too, of course. Not that you'd care about that."

Jared put his arms hard around her. "I'm going to take you home. Right now."

She longed to be home, lying in her own bed. Alone. "You are not. I'm not spoiling this evening for my mother just because of you. And if anyone takes me home, Patrick will."

The emotion Jared felt now was full-fledged jealousy. "You and I aren't through with each other," he grated, and felt a shudder run through her body.

She hated him, he thought, his shoulder muscles tightening another notch. Couldn't wait to be rid of him. No amount of apologizing was going to fix that. For once, he wasn't going to get what he wanted. Because what he wanted—on any terms at all—was Devon.

Which, he decided grimly, had damn well better be his final insight of the evening.

The pasta, blessedly, seemed to settle Devon's stomach. She danced with Benson, listened to the saga of the varicose veins, and had an entirely civil conversation with Lise. She also danced several times with Patrick. Patrick, in his usual state of dishabille, trundled her around the floor with the enthusiasm and idiosyncratic sense of rhythm his mother exhibited at the organ. They discussed molybdenum mining, the contenders for the Grey Cup, and their travels in the north. Patrick was a nice man, Devon thought, gazing at the splotch of soup on his tie. But not in a million years would she ever fall in love with him. Would this interminable evening never be over?

The only bright spot was that Jared hadn't asked her to dance again.

Trying to keep her toes out of reach of Patrick's overly large feet, she let her thoughts circle once again around her dilemma. The only plan she'd come up with was to watch Benson and Alicia all evening, and see if she could scout

out any cracks in their marriage. If Alicia divorced again, then Devon wouldn't be bound to her child's father or grandfather. She'd have, minimally, a little more freedom. She hated herself for thinking this way, but it was her only option.

However, Benson and Alicia were completely at ease with each other in a way that at any other time would have fascinated her. Alicia had been swept off her feet by the romantic Italian, overawed by the earl, and overpowered by the Texas oil baron, who'd had a very loud voice. Alicia and Benson's mutual pleasure in each other was both new and touching. Alicia and Benson, unless Devon was much mistaken, were going to be around for quite a while.

It was ironic that just when Devon wanted a convenient divorce she wasn't going to get it. Which left her thoughts fruitlessly circling the paths she'd worn bare the last few days. Abortion, adoption, marriage…abortion, adoption, marriage.

All of them equally impossible.

She glanced over at Jared and Lise, who were dancing only a few feet away, Lise clinging to Jared like glue. The neckline of Lise's suit needed to make acquaintance with a sewing machine, Devon thought shrewishly. Not that she cared. Jared and Lise deserved each other.

Her mind made a quick leap. What if Jared married Lise? Wouldn't that leave her, Devon, less frightened of the future? Less threatened by Jared? Of course it would.

The thought of telling Jared she was going to bear his child petrified her. But the thought of Lise in Jared's bed, night after night, roused a tumult of emotion in her breast that was almost more than she could bear. As Patrick led her back to the table, Devon saw the waiter approach Alicia and present her with the bill. Thank goodness. She could go home. Stop pretending that there was nothing wrong with her that rest and chicken soup wouldn't cure.

"Ready to leave, Devon?" Patrick asked.

She smiled at him in immense relief. For a few moments in the cab on their way over here, she'd been tempted to tell Patrick about her pregnancy. But Patrick was leaving at the end of the week to spend three weeks on northern Ellesmere. Why tell him? What good would it do?

Maybe she could go to the Arctic with him. That would put several thousand miles between her and Jared.

Quickly Devon embarked on a round of goodbyes, kissing her mother and Benson, exchanging pleasantries with the rest. Jared said, an undertone of savagery in his voice, "Goodbye, Devon. I'll see you at 'The Oaks' at Thanksgiving."

Thanksgiving was the last weekend of her vacation. She flew to Calgary the following week. Short of outright rudeness, there was no way Devon could get out of a weekend at "The Oaks."

She said with blatant insincerity, "I'll look forward to it," and watched his mouth tighten.

She was going to have to tell him. Sooner or later. The inevitable changes in her body would look after that.

Never in her life had she dreaded anything so much.

"The Oaks" in mid-October was breathtakingly beautiful. The grass was still a glossy green. The leaves on the oak trees were burnished like leather, the maples flaunted scarlet banners, and the birches showered thin gold medallions through their silvered branches. Even the light seemed saturated with gold, the air smelling deliciously of colder nights and crisp, fallen leaves.

Jared wasn't arriving until Sunday morning, so Alicia informed Devon. Which meant, in theory, that Devon had two days to enjoy herself before he came. She was now two and a half months pregnant. Her so-called morning sickness was almost gone, and the disconcerting fits of dizziness had passed altogether. She had a little color back in her cheeks; Alicia was patently relieved, although still determined to coddle her daughter.

On Friday afternoon Benson took her on a long tour of the barns and meadows; having seen her ride in the ring, he told her she could take any horse in the stables whenever she wanted. Since Devon kept to a rigorous daily exercise schedule no matter where she was in the world, and since she knew without vanity that she was an expert horsewoman, she wasn't worried that riding would in any way endanger her pregnancy. Late Friday afternoon and twice on Saturday Devon rode along the woodland trails that surrounded the fenced fields, and galloped across the unfenced meadows, getting her bearings and as always finding comfort in the unspoken rapport that existed between her and her mount.

The exercise did her good. She went to bed at ten on Saturday evening, and fell asleep right away. But at twenty after one in the morning she was wide awake, staring into the darkness. Jared would arrive today. She'd have to tell him she was pregnant.

Panic curled its way round her heart. Her life, arranged to keep intimacy and emotion at bay, was falling apart around her. All because of her own carelessness.

Because, too, of a man's fierce kisses and fiercer desire.

Oh, God, what was she going to do?

She could emigrate to Australia. Have the baby and pray it wouldn't look like Jared. But Alicia and Benson would be sure to come and visit her. Besides, she was ninety-nine percent sure Jared's genes would predominate, that her child, boy or girl, would have midnight-blue eyes and a crop of black hair.

Scratch Australia.

She could lie to Jared. Tell him the child was another man's, not his. That it had been conceived in Borneo or

Timbuktu. Deceive him as grievously as he'd deceived her in New York. That whole night she'd spent in his arms had been a lie.

But if she were to lie to him now, wouldn't that make her just like him? Manipulative and untrustworthy? She wasn't going to do that. She'd tell the truth. Not because she owed him anything; rather because she owed it to herself. No matter what the consequences.

The only other option was to wait until Christmas. By then she'd be five months pregnant and wouldn't have to say a word: just by looking at her everyone would know.

No, it had to be this weekend. Offense, so she'd learned in her years of negotiations, was almost always the best defense.

In a flurry of sheets, Devon got out of bed. She'd made one decision, at least: she wasn't going to toss and turn half the night, getting into a state. She'd go to the kitchen and make herself a sandwich. Her appetite seemed to be making up for lost time now that the nausea had abated.

A peanut butter and Cheese Whiz sandwich. With black olives.

And a glass of milk for calcium.

She padded downstairs into the kitchen. Impossible not to remember her and Jared munching on hamburgers the night of the wedding. Impossible to forget how wantonly she'd made love with him. Biting her lip, she opened the huge refrigerator, and five minutes later was perched on a stool chewing on an olive.

She had all the classic symptoms of pregnancy, she thought, including cravings for things like black olives and gingerbread slathered with whipped cream. Maybe if she spoke to the cook, they could have gingerbread for dessert tomorrow night.

When Jared was here.

The door creaked. As Devon stifled a cry of alarm, it

swung open and Jared stepped into the kitchen. As if she'd conjured him up, thought Devon, her sandwich poised halfway to her mouth. Not until she saw him did she realize how strongly she'd been hoping he'd be delayed. Or change his mind and not come at all.

He said, "I rather thought it might be you."

He was wearing a white shirt and tie, the jacket of his business suit slung over his arm. His big body seemed to fill the doorway. Devon mumbled, "You're not supposed to get here until tomorrow."

"Sorry to disappoint you," he answered curtly.

She yanked at the hem of her oversize T-shirt, which when she was standing reached almost to her knees but which right now was baring her thighs. "Party Animal," it announced in neon pink letters across her chest.

Jared stepped closer. She scrambled awkwardly to her feet, plunking her sandwich on the plate beside the bottle of olives; her breasts bounced under her shirt. He said, "You turn your nose up at Italian cuisine and now you're eating peanut butter?"

She hated the mockery in his voice. "I was hungry," Devon said stonily.

He reached out and took a strand of her hair, rubbing it between his fingers. She flinched back. "Don't, Jared! Please..."

His hand dropped to his side and his face hardened. "You can't stand the sight of me, can you?"

What she couldn't stand was for him to touch her. Because the odds were she'd melt in his arms and kiss him as though there was no tomorrow, and how could she maintain any self-respect that way? She said steadily, "You're catching on."

He hauled on the knot of his tie, loosening it with vicious strength. "Then why don't you vamoose?" he said unpleasantly. "Because I'm hungry, too, and I don't want to share the kitchen with a woman who treats me like a potential rapist.''

Devon grabbed her plate and glass of milk. ''Any more than I want to share it with a man who thinks women are the lowest form of life.''

''I apologized about the money!''

''Words come cheap, Jared.''

Cheap. He didn't like that word being applied to him, especially not by Devon. He grated, ''New York—what I said to you that morning, the way I behaved—I shouldn't have done it. It was shortsighted of me.''

She raised her brows. ''Shortsighted? That's one way of looking at it.'' Then she headed for the door, her bare feet slapping the cold tiles.

His voice followed her. ''At least try and behave as though I'm a human being in front of your mother and my father, will you? Otherwise it's going to be the longest Thanksgiving on record.''

''Oh, by all means let's keep up appearances.''

''Don't push me too far, Devon,'' he said softly.

''Don't try and intimidate me,'' she flashed.

As Jared took two steps toward her, his face like a mask of steel, Devon shoved at the door and scurried up the back stairs. By the time she'd reached the hallway her anger had deserted her; slow tears were seeping down her cheeks. She felt utterly alone. Alone and defenceless.

Jared the enemy, and nowhere to hide.

CHAPTER EIGHT

SUNDAY Devon woke late, from a sleep riddled with nightmares. The sun was shining through the curtains. Suddenly she longed for the wind in her face, the thud of hooves beneath her: anything to take her mind off Jared. She'd ride Rajah, the big bay gelding whose dark eyes radiated both intelligence and a fiery spirit.

Rajah lived up to his name. The first five minutes Devon spent establishing that she, not Rajah, was the boss. After that, she settled down to enjoy herself, guiding him across the jumps in the ring, ending in a wild gallop across the north meadow. Crouched forward in the stirrups, she urged the horse over a wide ditch. He landed as smoothly as any show jumper, and raced toward the trees. For Devon everything was forgotten but the present moment. The wind in her face, the thud of hooves beneath her...

Regretfully, she collected Rajah into a more sedate canter; then, as the maples brushed her head with their low branches, to a trot. Rajah pricked his ears. Whinnying, he pranced a little, his mane tossing.

Another horse was galloping toward them: the magnificent black stallion named Starlight for the white blaze on his forehead. Jared was riding him. Could she never escape Jared? she thought in despair.

"Easy, boy, easy," she murmured, leaning forward to rub Rajah's ears. Rajah sidled restlessly under her calming hands; Rajah liked to gallop just as much as Devon did.

As Jared eased back on the reins, Starlight dropped to a canter. Then Jared brought him to a walk, knowing he should be reining in his own temper at the same time. But when he'd watched Devon take Rajah over the ditch, bent low over the gelding's neck, his heart had been in his mouth. Rajah, of all the horses in his father's stables next to Starlight, was the most spirited and difficult to control. Was Devon clean crazy? Or just reckless?

He pulled up alongside her. Her cheeks were flushed from the wind and her eyes were the brilliant blue he remembered so well. He said tightly, "Who gave you permission to ride that horse?"

"Your father. Who happens to own him."

"My father didn't give you permission to take Rajah over ditches at forty miles an hour. This isn't Texas—Rajah's a thoroughbred, not some cow pony. You could have broken your neck!"

As her hands tightened on the reins, Rajah skittered nervously beneath her. She snapped, "We aren't going to have a row on top of two highly volatile horses. Go away, Jared. I was enjoying myself until you came along."

Then she took her feet from the stirrups and swung to the ground. Ignoring Jared, she led Rajah toward the stream that meandered through the trees, looping the reins round her wrist while the horse drank.

Jared dismounted, tied Starlight to the nearest tree with a long enough rein that the stallion could crop the grass, and headed after Devon. And with each step he took, he fought for control. He was famous for his control. Hated and feared for it. Often he used it as a weapon. So why did it desert him whenever he was anywhere near Devon? She was only a woman, after all.

Only? Devon? Who was he kidding?

She saw him coming; she was glaring at him. "You can't take a hint, can you?" she said bitterly.

"You look a lot better," he heard himself say; it was not how he'd planned to begin.

"Until you came along, I was feeling better."

Jared gave a reluctant laugh. "We can trade insults like a couple of kids in the playground, Devon. Or we could try behaving like adults—in all honesty, it scared the hell out of me seeing you ride Rajah so recklessly."

She tied the reins round the nearest branch. "There was nothing reckless in the way I was riding."

"That horse is hard to handle!"

"That horse is peacefully cropping the grass by the stream and I, as you see, am in one piece."

"You don't give an inch, do you?" he grated.

"Not where you're concerned."

Stirring uneasily in the breeze, the maple leaves, blood-red, flame-orange, swirled behind her. She was wearing a pale yellow shirt tucked into skin-tight jodhpurs; her leather boots were well worn, clinging to her slender calves. Wanting nothing more than to take her in his arms and kiss her until neither one of them could breathe, Jared said roughly, "I'm glad you're feeling better." He hadn't planned to say that, either.

Devon stood very still. The stream burbled gently behind her; Jared was framed in the russet leaves of a beech, his jet-black hair disordered from his gallop. She had to tell him she was pregnant, Devon thought in desperation. She had to. So why not here, in this beautiful place where no one else would interrupt them?

She took a deep breath. Once she'd told him, there'd be no going back. The truth would be out in the open, as irretrievable, as irreversible as her own condition. She said, rattling off the words as if they meant nothing, were of no more significance than a grocery list or an airline booking, "The reason I'm feeling better is because I'm over the worst of the morning sickness."

There was a small, deadly silence. "Morning sickness?"

She'd never heard that note in Jared's voice before.

Knowing she had to finish what she'd started, Devon said, "Yes. I'm pregnant."

For a few seconds he said nothing, seconds that stretched like hours for Devon. Her knees felt as undependable as the water in the brook; she was shivering with nerves. Then he said, each word falling like a stone, "Who's the father?"

"You are. Of course."

"Of course?" he said silkily. "I don't know the first thing about you—you could be sleeping with a dozen other men."

"I told you it had been a long time for me."

"Remember the wedding, Devon? How dizzy you were when the scallops were put in front of you? Were you pregnant then?"

Appalled, she gaped at him. More than once, she'd tried to picture Jared's response to her news. But she'd never come up with this: an outright denial that the child could be his. "Jared, I was jet-lagged and emotionally overwrought that day. I was not pregnant!"

"Of course you're going to say that. I'm a lot richer than any of the other men in your life, I'm sure."

"Oh, stop it!" she cried. "There aren't any other men, and do you think I want to be pregnant by you? That I'm trying to trap you into marriage? Believe me, you're the last man on earth I'd ever want to marry."

His leather boots rustling in the leaves, he closed the gap between them, his face a rictus of fury. Quailing inwardly, Devon fought for breath. "So what are you going to do?" he said with icy precision. "Have a convenient abortion?"

She grabbed the nearest branch, his features wavering in her vision, and spoke the literal truth. "I don't know what I'm going to do."

"What's my role—to rescue you from that dilemma?"

"The child is yours. Any DNA test will tell you so."

His breath hissed between his teeth. "You said you were protected against pregnancy."

"I thought I was."

"How convenient. Do you know how much I'm worth, Devon?" He named a figure that made her blink. "Yeah...quite a bit, isn't it? You think you're the first woman to try and trap me into holy matrimony?"

In a sweep of pure rage, Devon blazed, "Keep your precious money! As I keep telling you, to the point of boredom, I don't want it. You believed me, or so you said. Which shows how much your word is worth. Nothing. Absolutely nothing. So just you listen to me, Jared Holt—I'll go away for a year. And when I come back I'll tell your father and my mother that the baby's father is from Australia. Or the jungles of Borneo. You'd just better pray it doesn't look like you, okay?"

Jared said, a peculiar look on his face, "It's their grandchild. The one they wanted."

"Go to the top of the class."

"We'll have to get married—there's no other choice."

"We are not getting married," she said ferociously. "You're supposed to be some kind of business genius; surely you can come up with a more original strategy than that?"

"For at least the last five generations, the Holt men have had black hair and dark blue eyes," he snarled. "I won't allow you to make a fool of me in public."

"And what if it's a girl? With blond hair? What do we do then? Have a quickie divorce?"

Lines scoring his cheeks, he said softly, "When we get married, there'll be no divorce."

She said in a surge of hope, "But that would be one way out of this, don't you see? We'll marry and get a divorce a year later—why didn't I think of that before?"

"So you can marry again?" Jared lashed.

"I don't want to marry anyone—for the first time or the second. How many times do I have to tell you that?"

"No child of mine is going to be brought up by a step-parent."

His eyes, she thought unwillingly, looked like those of a man in torment. "You had a stepmother, didn't you?"

"If I did, that's no—"

"What went wrong, Jared?"

His lips narrowed. "I'll tell you what went wrong," he rasped. "Beatrice hated my guts. She was so jealous of me that she sent me off at the age of six to a fancy boarding school where I got bullied by the big boys and I was so lonely and homesick I thought I'd die." Jared raked his fingers through his black hair. "My father was too wrapped up in her to have a clue what was going on, and I was too proud and too stubborn to tell him. And why the devil am I telling you this? I never talk about that time. Not to anyone."

"You just did. To me," Devon said. It was the first clue she'd received to the demons that drove Jared. In her mind's eye she could see a little black-haired boy backed against a wall, surrounded by the bigger boys, and despite her anger felt her heart ache for him.

"You make me break every goddamned rule in the book."

"And you hate me for it," she faltered, close to tears.

He took her by the elbows. "Tell me the truth—are you planning an abortion?"

She shook her head. "I couldn't," she said. "I couldn't do that." She saw his features relax infinitesimally. "I can't put the baby out for adoption, either. I'm going to keep it, Jared. I'll manage."

"Yes, you will. Because you'll be my wife."

She was trembling very lightly. "We mustn't do that. We hate each other; you know we do. And, if I'm to be honest, I don't want a divorce any more than you do. My mother had three of them, I know what it's like. I won't put a child of mine through that.''

He said harshly, ''So we'll get married until—how does it go?—death do us part.''

''Jared, we can't! Divorce is bad enough. But it's far worse to live in the same household with a man and a woman who can't stand each other. Like my mother and the Italian count. And then the English earl and the Texas oil baron. I loathed it! All the tensions and fights and infidelities. The unending court battles, all of them over money. You wonder why I go off like a firecracker every time you wave your money in front of me? It's because I've seen what money can do to people.'' She took a long, shuddering breath. ''I won't put my child through any of that; I refuse to.''

''It's our child, Devon. Ours. Are you forgetting that?''

She said with genuine desperation, ''Do you believe me, Jared? That it is your child, and that the pregnancy was truly a mistake? I didn't plan this—I'd have to be mad!''

''Everything in my background tells me not to believe you.''

Not until he spoke did Devon realize how deeply she'd longed for him to trust her. Her shoulders sagged. ''If we got married,'' she said in a low voice, ''we'd be tied to each other for life. It would be awful.''

The words forced themselves through his lips. ''Do you really hate me that much?''

She'd been scuffing at the ground with the toe of her boot. What she felt for Jared wasn't as simple as hatred. No, it was far more complex than that. Struggling to be as honest as she could, Devon said, ''You betrayed something basic that night in New York. So now I can't trust you— what you do or what you say. Trust's basic, too, Jared.'' She kicked at a rock. ''I don't know what I feel for you. I do know I can't bear the thought of being trapped in a loveless marriage.''

"We've got no choice.''

His voice was as hard as granite, and his face, when she looked up, was equally unyielding. He was offering no explanations for the night in New York, no apology. And no choice other than marriage...hadn't her lack of choice been the crux of the matter ever since the doctor had told her she was pregnant? Devon said in a rush, ''Would you want me to have an abortion?''

"No!''

The word had burst from him. With the smallest of smiles, she said, ''Well, that's something... Jared, let's go back to the house. We've got the rest of the weekend, maybe one of us will have a brainwave and figure a way out of all this.''

"You really don't want to marry me, do you?''

There hadn't been a trace of emotion in his voice. ''I can't take any more of this,'' Devon said thinly, and reached for the reins.

"You'll walk the horse back to the stables.''

"*What* did you say?''

"Devon, you're pregnant—you think I'm going to let you take every ditch between here and the house at a dead gallop? Or are you hoping you'll fall off and that'll solve all your problems?''

In pure rage Devon flared, ''Let's get something straight, Jared Holt. I'm not one of your employees and I don't have to take orders from you. I'm an extremely good rider, I'm physically fit, and the last thing I'd do is put my child in any jeopardy.'' Her face changed. With sudden urgency, she said, ''Is Starlight loose?''

As Jared swung round, she leaped into the saddle, finding the stirrups with the ease of long practise, and took Rajah in a wide loop around him and around Starlight, who was, of course, still tied to the tree. Then, at an easy canter, she headed back across the fields.

Jared wasn't long in catching up. She gave him a gamine grin over her shoulder and said cordially, "Oldest trick in the book—I didn't think you'd fall for it."

"And you knew I wouldn't risk chasing you, not when you're pregnant," he said smoothly. "Well done, Devon. You're quite a woman."

"Aren't I?" she said amiably. "Let me tell you something—I may be pregnant but I have no intentions of spending the next seven months reclining on a couch."

"Doing embroidery."

She gave a choke of laughter. "I don't even know which end of a needle is which."

He said evenly, "When's the baby due, Devon?"

The smile died from her face. "April."

"Have you told anyone else?"

"Of course not."

He muttered, "I wish I— Oh, to hell with all this. I'm going to take Starlight to the lake. I'll see you back at the house."

He dug his heels into Starlight's flanks. The stallion took off in a smooth surge of energy that was beautiful to watch. As Devon dissuaded Rajah from following, her eyes were glued to the man on the stallion's back. He, too, was beautiful to watch, she thought reluctantly. Hate him? No matter what he'd done, she didn't hate him.

But he'd soon grow to hate her, trapped in a marriage he didn't want with a child he hadn't planned for.

Married to Jared for the rest of her life? It was out of the question.

For the next twenty-four hours Devon was aware of Jared watching her. Watching her but making no attempt to talk to her about anything other than trivia. After a late brunch, the four of them went for a walk, gathering armloads of scarlet leaves to decorate the dining room, then Devon disappeared for a rest. Dinner was more formal; she wore a purple dress that swirled around her hips and ate her way through the menu. Jared didn't even try to detain her before she went to bed, and when she went for an early-morning ride he was nowhere to be seen.

But when she came downstairs after lunch, carrying her overnight bag, he was waiting for her in the hall. He said harshly, "Are you in Toronto next weekend?"

"I go to Calgary Wednesday. But I'm back on Friday."

"I'll meet you for lunch on Saturday—I'll be on my way to Hong Kong—and we'll talk. Give me your phone number."

Her hesitation must have been obvious to him. He said in a savage undertone, "You're carrying my child, Devon, and you're worrying about a phone number?"

My child...

She reeled off the numbers. Then, to her great relief, she heard Benson and Alicia coming to wish her goodbye. She hugged them both and kissed her mother. Jared gave her a formal nod; he'd disappeared by the time she drove away in her red Mazda.

My child... Did that mean Jared did believe her? But he hadn't as much as touched her all weekend. In spite of all their conflict, she'd wanted him to kiss her goodbye, even if it was only on the cheek. Or at the very least to take her hand, acknowledging in some way that their fates were bound together. Sex, she thought despairingly, winding between the white fences, was the only thing that might hold them together. The one place where, just possibly, they could meet.

If that was taken away, what was left?

Jared phoned on Friday evening, a conversation so brief and businesslike that Devon felt she was talking to a stranger. Since she couldn't imagine that anything she and Jared had to say would be suitable for a public place, she invited him to her condo for lunch. On Saturday morning she made carrot soup and bought crunchy rolls from the nearby bakery. Then she got dressed in tailored trousers with a crisp white shirt and an embroidered vest from Tibet, and pulled her hair back into a ruthlessly smooth braid. The waistband of the trousers was snug. Quelling pure panic, she set the table.

Promptly at noon the downstairs buzzer sounded and a few minutes later she opened the door to Jared. As he stepped across her threshold, she had the crazy sense that she was letting the enemy in. That her personal space, so important to her, was no longer inviolate.

Jared put his bags on the floor and handed her his coat. His suit was impeccably tailored. He looked exactly what he was: a powerful, sophisticated and ruthless man who, because of her carelessness, now had a hold over her. Still without saying a word, he handed her a florist's box.

Inside was a single exquisite spray of orchids, the petals a delicate pink, the centres carmine, frilled and sensual. "Why are you giving me this?" Devon said baldly.

"You stepped on the last lot."

The bouquet at the wedding. "So I did," Devon gulped. "Is that the only reason?"

"I don't know...I saw them in the window of the flower shop at the airport and they made me think of you."

"They're beautiful," she muttered, then flushed. "I didn't mean—"

"Not as beautiful as you," Jared said.

His dark eyes were fastened on her face; she ached to be held by him, to feel the comfort and strength and heat of his embrace. She said hastily, "I'll put them in water. Make yourself at home."

When she rejoined him, he was looking around with genuine interest. Her living room was high-ceilinged with tall windows; her few paintings and the sculptures she'd collected on her travels made clear statements against the ivory walls. An Indian silk carpet lay on the hardwood floor. He said appreciatively, "Space and light...it's a lovely room, Devon."

"Can I get you a glass of wine?"

"Thanks."

He was examining a small jade Buddha when she came back. "I don't have long," he said. "Maybe we could eat and talk?"

Had she been afraid that he'd sweep her off to bed and make glorious love to her? Not a chance, by the look of him. "Sure," Devon said, and fled to the kitchen. She served the soup, heated the rolls and put out the pâté and crisp vegetables she'd bought at the market. Then she sat down across from Jared.

For a moment he looked down at the steaming bowl of soup, decorated with parsley sprinkled on a swirl of sour cream, then he looked across at Devon. Her living space intrigued him; it took confidence and a clear sense of self to live with space. Lise's apartment was such a clutter of theater memorabilia that he felt stifled there.

He could have arrived here earlier this morning. But he knew himself well enough to realize that if he had, he'd have ended up in bed with Devon. The waters were muddied enough as it was. He couldn't afford to go to bed with her, no matter how much his body craved to do so. He took a sip of the soup, not surprised to find it exotically spiced, and said, "During the last few days I've had you investigated."

"You *what*?"

"They turned up a man called Peter Damien—you gave him the boot in May when you found out he was engaged—

and a cardiologist called Steve Danford seven years ago. No one else.''

Devon had had time to recover. She said coldly, ''The baby, in other words, is yours.''

''Right.'' He buttered a roll with a deliberation that set her teeth on edge. ''You were an excellent student and you're highly thought of at your office. Both the kids' drop-in center and the women's shelter sang your praises.'' His smile was mocking. ''A blameless life, Devon.''

''How reassuring for you.''

He said sharply, ''I'm being honest with you. I could have kept the investigation a secret.''

''You could have trusted me!''

He could have. She was right. ''I wasn't ready to. We'll get married at 'The Oaks' in two weeks. Our respective parents can be the witnesses and we'll pray Aunt Bessie doesn't get wind of it.''

Devon looked ready, he thought with wintry amusement, to dump her entire bowl of soup on his head. ''Have you taken it upon yourself to tell my mother?'' she flashed.

''I thought I'd leave that up to you. I'm out of the country for the next ten days.''

''And do I tell them I'm pregnant?''

He glanced at the curves of her breasts under her white shirt. ''I would think so. It's not something you're going to be able to hide.''

''I'm surprised you haven't tried to buy me off! As you did my mother.''

''What's the point, the way you feel about my money? Anyway, this isn't nearly as simple a situation. You're carrying my child, Devon. My son or my daughter.''

His voice sounded as though he was discussing commodity options; Devon's cheeks reddened with fury. ''If I could think of any other way out of this, I wouldn't even be sitting here,'' she flared. ''But I can't. I'm trapped.''

He might as well go for broke. "One more thing," Jared said. "Your job. Now that you're pregnant, I don't want you exposing yourself to all the risks of the tropics. And once the baby's born you won't be able to be away so much. You'd better hand in your notice."

Through gritted teeth, Devon said, "Oddly enough, I'd already thought of that. I can take a year's leave of absence with an option to do translation and interpretation when I go back. And how dare you try and run my life?"

He said with furious emphasis, "Why do you have to argue all the time?"

"So you won't swallow me alive," she announced, and tore off a hunk of roll, jabbing it with the butter knife.

She had a crumb on her lower lip. Her infinitely kissable lip. Jared kept his hands on his side of the table and said, "We'll take four or five days after the wedding and go down to the Bahamas."

"A honeymoon? No way!"

"I've said that's what we're doing, Devon."

Her fingers were trembling very lightly as she spread pâté on her bread. But when she spoke she sounded entirely self-possessed. "Controlling someone else's life can go two ways. Now it's my turn. I have a condition, Jared. A very simple one. But if you don't agree to it, the wedding's off."

He had no idea what it could be. Was that one of the reasons that Devon fascinated him? That she was so totally unpredictable? "Go ahead," he said.

"I'll expect you to be faithful to me. I won't tolerate Lise as your mistress."

"I accept that condition," he said curtly.

"You do?"

"In fact, I'd require the same thing of you. Dammit, Devon, the marriage vows have to mean something."

She looked straight at him; he noticed how the pulse at the base of her throat was throbbing beneath her creamy skin. In open challenge, she said, "To love and to cherish…what about that particular phrase? Or are you just picking out the ones that suit you?"

His fist clenched on the tablecloth. She deserved the truth from him, he thought, and said hoarsely, "I don't think I know how to fall in love with a woman. I never have. But I'll be faithful to you, I swear."

With an ache in his gut, he watched tears gather in her sea-blue eyes. If I touch her, I'm lost, he thought, and heard her say, "Then I'll marry you, Jared."

He said the first thing that came into his head. "I—I didn't get you a ring."

"I hate diamonds," she said forcefully.

"Then I won't get you diamonds," said Jared.

She scrubbed at her eyes with her napkin, smearing her eyeshadow. "You don't have to get me anything," she said. "There's fruit for dessert and I have three more trips I'm committed to before I can quit my job. Morocco next week, two conferences in London, and a quick flight to Baffin Island."

She looked as rebellious as any teenager, he thought, with a rush of emotion he labeled amusement but that felt far more complicated and confusing. He'd be worried sick each time until she landed safely back in Toronto. Worried? Jared Holt? He never worried about anyone; it was a policy of his.

He pushed back his cuff and glanced at his watch. "I'd better skip the fruit…the limo's picking me up in five minutes. I'll be in touch once you're back from Morocco." With a straight face he added, "Wonderful soup…I'm glad you can cook."

Swift laughter shimmered in her irises; her mood changes were another of the things that drew him to her. She stood up and accompanied him to the door, taking his coat out of the closet. "Thank you again for the orchids," she said.

Had he ever wanted to kiss a woman as badly as he now wanted to kiss Devon? "Take care," he said brusquely.

"You, too."

The light had gone from her eyes. Run for your life, Jared, he thought, opened the door and shut it decisively behind him.

He'd gotten out of there without taking her to bed. Without even touching her. And it had half killed him.

CHAPTER NINE

HER wedding day.

Devon lay in bed at "The Oaks," in the same room she'd been given when her mother had married Benson last summer. It was now November, never her favorite month. It was, by the sound of it, raining.

At one o'clock she and Jared were getting married. Benson and Alicia were to be the witnesses, and Benson had insisted on inviting Aunt Bessie and Uncle Leonard. After a celebratory lunch—Alicia's phrase—Jared and Devon were driving to Toronto and flying to the Bahamas, to a new resort that Jared owned in the Exumas, for a four-day honeymoon. From there they were jetting to Vancouver, where they were to live in a house Jared already owned—the house he'd been meaning to settle down in for a couple of years. He would use the house as a base, commuting to New York, the Far East, and wherever else the demands of business required his presence.

To all this Devon had acquiesced. Her agreement to marry Jared, she thought, had been like a small rock sitting at the top of a hillside about to start a landslide. She herself was now tumbling down the slope, end over end. Out of control.

Her year's leave of absence had been approved at company headquarters. She'd let out her condo because the real estate market was in a slump and she didn't want to take a loss; besides, at some level, she wasn't ready to sell it. Her furniture, her paintings, and her red Mazda were on their way to Vancouver. After she'd come back from Morocco, the Toronto office had thrown a very nice party for her, which Jared had been unable to attend; he'd been in Hawaii, on his way home from Hong Kong.

Step by step, she'd cut herself off from her former life, organizing everything to fit in with Jared's demands, Jared's job, Jared's house in Vancouver. Jared's baby, she thought unhappily. The result of Jared's ill-judged affair with her. If she'd been in any doubt before, she now knew why he was the head of a multimillion dollar business empire. It was because, once he'd made up his mind to a course of action, he was ruthlessly efficient and brooked no argument in carrying it out.

Her pregnancy seemed to have reached the stage where all she wanted to do was sleep. She was too tired to fight him any more. It was easier just to go along with him. Leave her job. Get married. Live in Outer Mongolia. Have triplets if that was what he wanted. What was the difference?

She felt paralyzed, immobilized, shut down. Like a dummy in a store window. Or a doll in a toy shop, the kind that produced a rote message every time you pressed a button in its back. Yes, Jared. No, Jared. Whatever you say, Jared.

What was the matter with her? She'd never been one to lie down to the blows of fate. She wouldn't have gotten her job, or done it so well, if she'd gone around being passive and agreeable to everyone. She'd always been a fighter.

But there was no point in fighting Jared. She'd tried. And she'd lost.

I'm living in a dream, Devon thought. But I'm not writing the plot. Jared is.

And what would she do if she were to wake up? If she had any sense, she'd run down to the stables, get on Rajah and gallop full speed into the sunset. Except that it was pouring with rain and there wouldn't be any sunset, and by this evening she'd be married anyway.

It was too late to run away.

Devon curled up in a ball, pulling the covers over her head. Too many people were involved for her to run away. The day after Jared had left for Hong Kong, she'd invited Benson and Alicia for supper. She'd served them the remains of the carrot soup for the first course, she remembered with a wry smile; Alicia had complimented her on its flavour. To which Devon had blurted, "Jared and I are getting married."

"What?" Alicia had cried.

"Why?" Benson had demanded.

Devon had stirred her soup, watching the sour cream sink below the surface. "In two weeks. At 'The Oaks,' if that's okay with both of you."

"Darling," Alicia cried, getting up and kissing her daughter on the cheek, "of course it is. I'm very happy for you. Love at first sight—and I hadn't even noticed."

Benson said sharply, "I didn't think the two of you were even remotely compatible."

"Oh, yes," Devon lied valiantly. "It just took us a while to figure it out." All her carefully rehearsed speeches abandoned her. As her spoon trailed parsley flakes, she added in a rush, "I'm pregnant. With your grandchild."

For once, Alicia was speechless. Benson said with a careful lack of emphasis, "Are you in love with Jared, Devon?"

"I will be. Given time," she said, ducking her chin still further to her chest.

"And he with you?"

"You'll have to ask him that," she replied with a flicker of defiance.

Benson said abruptly, "I failed Jared once. When he was very young. Failed him badly, which I'm convinced is part of the reason he's so withdrawn, so cynical about women. You don't know how often I've wished I could undo the past, remedy my own blindness and stupidity…but I can't do that. None of us can.''

Devon said, ''He told me about Beatrice.''

''He did?'' Benson paused, eying her shrewdly. ''How interesting—he refuses pointblank to talk to me about her. If he's opened up to you like that, Devon, then maybe you are the right woman for him.''

I don't think so.

Fortunately, Devon hadn't spoken those words out loud. But as she turned over in bed on this rainy morning in November, burying her face in the pillow, she didn't think she was the right woman for Jared at all.

He'd scarcely laid a finger on her since she'd told him about the pregnancy. As though she disgusted him. As though by trapping him into marriage, a marriage he'd never wanted, she was no longer the object of his desire. He didn't want to marry her. He didn't want her in his bed.

Four days alone with him? She was dreading it.

A tap came at the door. ''Darling, are you awake?''

Devon forced her lips into the semblance of a smile. ''Come in, Mother.''

''I brought you breakfast,'' Alicia said perkily.

The tray was charmingly laid with a starched cloth and a white rose in a silver vase. Touched, Devon said, ''That's sweet of you.''

''Devon, I do so hope you'll be happy. I want you to be as happy with Benson's son as I am with Benson.''

Alicia had clearly rehearsed this little speech. Knowing she mustn't start to cry, because if she did she might not be able to stop, Devon said, ''Thanks, Mother. I'm sure I will be.''

''He apologized, you know. Jared, I mean. For trying to bribe me not to marry his father. He said he shouldn't have done it, he was very sorry, and he could see how well suited we were. It was after you'd left at Thanksgiving.''

"He did?" Devon said blankly.

"He wasn't what you'd call effusive—I don't suppose Jared is used to apologizing for anything," Alicia said, her head on one side. "But he meant it, I'm sure…I don't think he does anything he doesn't want to do."

Except marry me, thought Devon.

"Benson told me about Beatrice," Alicia went on. "A witch, darling, a positive witch, and pathologically jealous. She hated Jared on two counts—he was another woman's son, and Benson loved him. I'm convinced that's why Benson wants a grandchild. So he can do a better job the next time round."

"I'm glad Jared apologized," Devon said, and felt her heart lighten by the smallest of degrees.

"You're just what he needs, darling."

If only he thought so. But Devon couldn't say that.

After breakfast, she finished packing for her honeymoon, had a leisurely bath and got dressed. She was wearing silk, always her favorite fabric, fashioned this time into a simple skirt and tunic that flowed subtly over her curves. It was white. She might not be a virgin, she thought ruefully, but she sure felt like one.

At twelve-thirty Martin, the butler, delivered a small box to her door. "Flown in for you this morning, madam," he said. The box contained a single exquisite orchid; the card said simply, "Jared."

Why would he say "love"? This marriage wasn't about love.

Ignoring the ache in her heart, Devon pinned the flower to her hair and applied blusher to her cheeks to give herself some color. Then, her face a perfectly controlled mask, she walked downstairs.

Alicia, cheated of a society wedding, had filled the living room with flowers, so many flowers it was almost impossible to see the sodden, leaf-bare garden through the windows. A fire danced in the hearth. Six people were clustered round it, waiting for her. Uncle Leonard and Aunt Bessie, the latter in an acid-green dress that was too tight for her, Benson, Alicia, the clergyman who had married them, and Jared. Jared was wearing a formal business suit; he looked forbiddingly severe, not at all like a prospective groom happily waiting for his bride.

Devon's fears, if anything, intensified. Nevertheless, as she watched Jared's taut profile, she suddenly wished she'd ordered a flower for his lapel. Any kind of flower. In swift compunction, she realized it hadn't even occurred to her.

He'd had an orchid ordered specially for her, and delivered to her door.

None of them had noticed her. Swiftly she retreated, and from the bouquet that stood just outside the door she extracted a single rosebud. She tiptoed down the corridor to the kitchen, asked Martin for a knife, and cut most of the stem off. It was a peach-pink rose, a color very sure of itself. Very much alive.

Darn it, she wasn't going to her own wedding like a lamb to the slaughter, Devon thought, gazing into the tightly furled petals as if somehow they could speak to her. Jared had apologized to Alicia, admitted he'd done a wrong. And all his passion toward herself, which had changed her into a woman fully alive and wondrously responsive, couldn't simply have disappeared. It had gone underground, maybe. But it was still there. After all, hadn't he given her the orchid now nestled in her hair? She'd always considered orchids very sexy flowers.

She went back to the living room, her head held high. As her heels tapped on the oak floor, Jared turned around. Clutching the rosebud as if it were a talisman, she smiled at him. Then she walked right up to him, took his lapel and inserted the stem through the small buttonhole. The rose lopped sideways. Her tongue between her teeth, Devon tugged on it. "It's not cooperating," she muttered, "I should have brought a pin."

Alicia said, "Wait a moment, darling, I'll get one."

Feeling rather foolish, Devon stayed where she was; she could smell Jared's aftershave, painfully familiar to her. He was standing very still. When she glanced up, his dark blue eyes were looking down at her, their expression unreadable. "I like the color," he said.

"Of the rose? Or my dress?" she said impishly, and was impressed with how at ease she sounded.

"Both, of course." His voice deepened. "You look very beautiful."

"Thank you," Devon whispered, and heard Alicia come back into the room. Devon took the pin from her, anchored the rosebud to Jared's lapel and stood back. "That's better," she said with great satisfaction.

A smile was lurking on Jared's face. "Shall we start?"

She took her place by his side, Benson on her other side. Sparks shot from the fireplace, and she could still see the rose from the corner of her eye. But as she promised to love and cherish Jared her voice trembled, and her fingers trembled as she eased the ring she had chosen for him over his finger. It was a plain gold band; inside, she'd had inscribed, "My third gift for you."

Now, she was wishing she hadn't. That she'd left the ring plain and unadorned.

"I pronounce you man and wife," the clergyman said, and smiled at the two of them. "You may kiss the bride," he said to Jared.

Devon's breath caught in her throat as Jared bent his head. His lips were firm and warm; the contact shivered through her. Then, almost immediately, he drew back.

Alicia and Benson kissed her, Alicia kissed Jared, and Benson gave his son a rough hug. Aunt Bessie said as smugly as if she herself was personally responsible for the marriage, "I knew at Benson's wedding that you'd met your match, Jared. You need a woman who'll keep you in line. I keep Leonard in line, don't I, honey?"

"All the time," Leonard said, and winked at Devon.

Leonard, Devon was quite sure, had never tried to step out of line. "Too bad there wasn't an organ," Leonard added piously.

Somewhat cheered, Devon glanced over at Jared. It's done, she thought. I'm Jared's wife. For the rest of my life.

She couldn't begin to fathom what those words meant.

She tried to enjoy herself—she talked too much and too fast, she laughed and ate. And all the while her brain and her heart were struggling to comprehend what she'd done in marrying Jared. Fashioned for herself an elaborate and expensively furnished trap? Or—by some remote chance— given herself a doorway through which she might pass into a true and loving relationship?

If only she and Jared could fall in love... For a split second a vision of such serendipity flooded Devon's mind that she totally lost track of the conversation eddying around her. "Devon?" Jared was saying quizzically, "what do you think?"

I think it would make me happy beyond anything I've ever known... She flushed scarlet and stammered, "S-sorry, I wasn't listening."

Jared in love with her? Or she with him? She was losing it.

She struggled to pay attention. Then, all too soon, it was time to leave. Benson and Alicia drove them to the airport. At the security gate, Alicia produced a few decorative but very sincere tears, and Benson said gruffly, "I'm glad you've married my son, Devon...be happy."

Then Jared and Devon passed through the barrier. The two of them, thought Devon. No one else.

She could think of nothing to say, and Jared was similarly immersed in silence as they walked what felt like miles to get to the area of the terminal where his company jet was parked. They boarded with a minimum of fuss, Devon responding appropriately to the congratulations of the crew members. The jet taxied down the runway, waited for clearance and took off. Jared said, "If you don't mind, Devon, there's some paperwork I should deal with before we get there."

"No problem," she said, leaned back in her seat and closed her eyes. With them shut, she could pretend she was alone. And almost believe it...

She woke about half an hour before the landing, going to the luxuriously appointed bathroom to repair her make-up. When she got back to her seat, Jared was still absorbed in a sheaf of papers, typing the occasional note into a lap-top, and didn't even acknowledge her presence. Perhaps he planned to work the whole four days, she thought wildly, and gazed out the window at the sun setting in gaudy splendor over a sea like stained glass. The colors reminded her of the rose Jared was still wearing in his lapel.

She'd certainly suffered from prenuptial nerves. But her nervous system was now on red alert, she thought unhappily, as she caught the first glimpse of the white-circled, mountainous islands that were their destination. In Nassau they changed to a company helicopter, which whirled them forty miles south to the Exumas, landing on a small island east of Great Exuma, an island that Jared owned outright.

A car was waiting for them; they drove only a few minutes, pulling up in front of a low bungalow separated from the rest of the resort complex by a stretch of palm trees, a tall gate and stone walls tumbling with vivid bougainvillea. As the driver carried their bags in, Devon hurried indoors; she didn't want Jared to carry her over the threshold, as if, indeed, a true marriage was about to begin. She didn't think she could bear that.

The floor was a cool, pale tile, the walls a delicate green, the furniture an attractive mix of bamboo and teak. Jared said levelly, "Make yourself at home, Devon. I've got a couple of calls to make, then why don't we eat outside? Marisha said she'd leave something for us in the refrigerator."

His mind, she could tell, was elsewhere. Not on her at all. Feeling as though she was bleeding inside, Devon replied without a trace of sarcasm, "Whatever you say."

Jared gave her a sharp look. "I have to clear this up," he said brusquely. "It won't keep. But it won't take long."

"Just so long as you have your priorities straight."

She hadn't meant to say that. A frown dug furrows into his brow. "What are you getting at, Devon?" he said with menacing softness.

"Hadn't you better make your call? I wouldn't want our first marital dispute to get in the way of Holt Incorporated."

"Holt Incorporated pays for everything around you...or had you forgotten that?"

"You can't buy me, Jared!"

"You're spoiling for a fight, aren't you? I'll be glad to oblige—once I've made my calls. They're important."

And I'm not.

"Fine," she said and kicked off her white pumps. "Barefoot, pregnant, and in the kitchen—that's where I belong. How very traditional of you."

"Maybe it's time I clarify something," Jared said with deadly precision. "One of my unbreakable rules is never to allow a woman to come between me and business. Nobody—but nobody—does that. Do you understand?"

"It would be difficult not to, wouldn't it?" she retorted. Then she stalked out of the room on her stockinged feet. Jared didn't come after her.

The refrigerator had enough food for a dozen honeymoons, and Devon wasn't the least bit hungry. She'd won-

dered in the few moments before she'd gone to sleep on
the plane if Jared would fall on her as soon as they were
alone, as he had in New York. Obviously not, she thought,
marching from room to room. The bathroom had a Jacuzzi
and heaps of thick, fluffy towels, the bedroom was bigger
than her living room at home and the bed was enormous.

Devon averted her eyes and scurried into the dining area,
which opened onto a patio that led into an enclosed garden.
The garden furniture was also teak, sheltered under a trellis
laden with vines. She could hear Jared talking to someone
on the phone.

He sounded a million miles away. He probably wanted
to be a million miles away. For sure, he didn't want to be
here, with her. Her brief spurt of anger fizzled away, leaving a pain that frightened her with its intensity. She stumbled outside, leaving the doors open. The sky glittered with
stars, points of light as far away and impersonal as Jared.
The air was saturated with the sweetness of frangipani and
the salt tang of the ocean, whose waves she could hear
gently laving the shore.

A swimming pool, smooth as silk, reflected the tiny stars
and the shimmer of a new moon. A froth of white bougainvillea cascaded down the walls at the back of the garden. And then Devon saw the gate.

It must be a gate to the beach. She could, even if only
for a while, escape.

It wasn't until then that she realized how claustrophobic
she was finding this beautiful walled garden. How like a
prison. She padded the length of the pool and grabbed the
big iron handle. But it turned only so far, and the gate
stayed shut.

Devon turned the handle again and again, shoving
against the thick wood boards with all her strength, suddenly desperate to get out. She thumped her shoulder

against the unyielding panels. And only then did she notice the iron key hole set higher in the door.

The door was locked. But there was no key.

She pounded her fists on the wood in helpless frustration, dimly aware that tears were streaming down her face. Then, slowly, she sank to the ground, her forehead resting against the boards, and wept as though her heart would break.

Jared said goodbye with complete civility and banged the receiver back into its cradle. As he'd half expected, Michaels had fouled up on the commodity transfers. Michaels, he thought grimly, was very soon going to find himself demoted. Jared didn't believe in carrying dead wood.

He shoved his papers in his leather briefcase, threw his jacket and tie over the chair, and decided he needed a drink. Abruptly aware of the silence, he called out Devon's name.

She didn't answer. Sulking, he thought irritably. He couldn't stand being interrupted when business was on his mind, the sooner she learned that, the better. But before he could leave the room, he noticed from the corner of his eye the rosebud dangling from the lapel of his jacket. Moved by an impulse he didn't understand, he unpinned it, poured water into a glass on the bureau, and stuck the rose in it. Then he strode into the kitchen.

The refrigerator door was firmly shut, and the kitchen was empty. Swiftly he went into the bedroom. Devon's cases were exactly where the driver had left them; there was no other sign of her occupancy.

Jared felt the first twinge of alarm. She wouldn't have gone swimming. Not without getting changed. "Devon!" he called, and listened to the silence echo in his ears.

The garden. Of course. She'd been cooped up all day; she'd gone into the garden. The patio doors were open, the pool an unbroken sheen under the stars. The water looked depthless, sinister; for a moment sheer terror flicked through him. And then, with a jolt in his gut, he saw the white figure slumped, ghostlike, on the ground by the gate.

Was she hurt? What was wrong?

He ran the length of the pool and hunkered down beside her, in one swift glance taking in the desolate hunch of her shoulders and the defeated curve of her nape. Only then did he realize that she was weeping, silently, in utter despair.

For a moment Jared was paralyzed, unable to think of anything to do or say. Devon wasn't a woman who wept for effect, he knew that already. Her tears were real, from the heart; they smote him in a place deep inside, a place he'd kept so well-protected for so many years that no one ever reached him there.

Until now.

Clumsily he took her by the shoulders, trying to see into her face. She resisted him, beating at his chest with her fists, her hair falling forward to hide her features. "Go away," she sobbed. "Go away and leave me alone…"

"Devon, what's wrong?" Brilliant question, Jared. No wonder you're the president of the company.

She twisted away from him. "I wish I'd never met you, never gone to bed with you… Oh, God, what have we done? We should never have got married."

Her words were as deadly sharp as the spines on the sea urchins near the reef, spines that were filled with poison. She didn't want to be married to him. Less than eight hours after the wedding and she was crying her eyes out because she'd made a terrible mistake.

He was the one who'd forced the marriage. Who'd made mincemeat out of all her objections and her doubts, and overridden any possibility of alternate solutions. He'd gotten her on his terms. He always got women on his terms.

His whole life was on his terms. Yet for the very first time in his life, victory tasted like ashes on Jared's tongue.

What was the use of being married to Devon if she was like a bird battering its wings against the bars of the cage, frantic to escape?

So what if the cage was gilded? Devon didn't want his money. She was too independent, too gutsy, too...too much Devon, he thought with painful honesty. Except that right now she didn't look either independent or gutsy. She looked broken.

Broken. He'd done that. His responsibility. He'd tamed her, just as he'd threatened to do.

What are you going to do for an encore, Jared? Hide behind the fax machine? Invent an international crisis and fly off to New York? Or are you going to tell her everything'll be fine? Here, Devon, take two aspirins and go to bed.

Bed. He couldn't afford to think about Devon in bed. Not now. But equally he couldn't afford to retreat behind his famous self-control. Control was out if he wanted Devon to stop that terrible, silent weeping. Useless to him and to her.

Then Jared's thoughts made another leap. Hadn't he wished, more than once, that just one woman would take him for himself, regardless of his money? Take him for the man he was, not for a rich man. Devon didn't care about his money. So now it was up to him to show her the man behind the money, the man who'd been in hiding for as long as he could remember.

New territory. A whole new venture.

Did he really want to do that?

CHAPTER TEN

JARED took a deep breath, rested one hand on Devon's shoulder and muttered, "Devon, I hate seeing you cry...tell me what to do."

She banged her palm against the gate. "There's nothing you can do. It's too late, don't you *see*?"

The wedding band he'd given her shone coldly on her finger. Praying for wisdom, Jared said, "I'm going to carry you into the house. You can have a hot bath and then I'm going to feed you oatmeal. With raisins and cream and lots of sugar. Comfort food. It's never too late for oatmeal, Devon."

She scrubbed at her face with her other hand and for the first time looked right at him. "Oatmeal?" she cried. "I'm telling you we've just made the worst mistake in our whole lives and you're talking about oatmeal?"

Feeling the words like stones in his throat, knowing he was going somewhere he'd never gone before, Jared said, "Whenever Beatrice punished me for doing something I hadn't even realized was wrong—this was before I was sent to boarding school—the housekeeper, Mrs. Baxter, used to feed me oatmeal and cream in the kitchen of her cottage, and let me pet her cat." Briefly he looked beyond Devon into the secluded darkness of the garden. "He was a spectacularly ugly orange tomcat called Turnip, and I loved him. Beatrice ran over him one day, in the driveway. An accident, she said."

"Oh, Jared..."

"I can't stand seeing you weep," he repeated with suppressed vehemence.

138

"Have you ever told anyone else about the tomcat?" Devon whispered.

"Of course not. What would I do that for?"

"Thank you for telling me."

He rubbed his jaw; it was tight with tension. "Oatmeal, Devon. My best offer."

"In that case," she said unsteadily, "I'd better take it."

She was smiling, Jared saw with a lurch of his heart. Very gently he rubbed the tears from her cheeks. "I make very good oatmeal. My one claim to culinary fame."

"I like lots of raisins."

They were using the words as a bridge, he thought, to carry them from a place of too much emotion back to the mundane. That was okay with him. Telling her all that stuff about Beatrice...what had possessed him? Beatrice was long gone. Nothing to do with Devon. He braced himself and gathered her in his arms, then lifted her. "You're no lightweight," he grumbled. Anything to hide the effect of her scent, her arm so soft around his neck, her closeness after what felt like months of deprivation.

"You're no romantic," she teased.

"That's because you scare me half to death," he said, not joking.

Devon stared up at him. "Would you mind repeating that?"

"I would mind." He walked through the dining room and put her down in the bathroom. "I'll bring your case in," he said, not looking at her because if he did he'd start kissing her and he wouldn't be able to stop.

"Thank you," Devon said uncertainly, and watched him go. She had no idea what was going on. She did know her frantic need for escape had vanished. Jared had feelings, she thought. But he'd shoved them all underground years ago because of a woman called Beatrice. If he hadn't found

her, Devon, weeping like that, he'd never have told her
about Turnip the tomcat and the oatmeal.

Jared put her case down on the bathroom floor, turned
on his heel and smartly shut the door. Scared of her? Jared?
Could it possibly be true?

Frowning in thought, Devon walked over to the mirror.
She looked a fright, she thought dispassionately. She was
too fair-skinned to cry with any pretensions to beauty: her
nose was red and her cheeks splotchy. A shower. A very
fast shower. Maybe she'd put on that sexy nightdress she'd
bought in a boutique in the Lanes. If she had the nerve.

Five minutes later, her heart in her mouth, Devon padded
barefoot into the kitchen.

Jared looked up. The saucepan, full of dried oatmeal and
raisins, slipped from his hand and clattered onto the tile
floor. Devon was standing in the doorway as naked as the
day she was born, her eyes wide-held. *"Devon..."* he
croaked.

"We could have oatmeal afterward."

Her voice was high-pitched with nervousness. In the light
from the two wall lamps the curves of her body flowed one
into the other; there were faint shadows under her breasts,
and beneath her collarbones. She wasn't posing, or trying
to be seductive, Jared thought. In fact, the exact opposite.
She looked as if she was on her way to the stake.

If he was scared of her, so was she of him, he realized
in a flash of insight. And finally Jared knew what to do.
The time was right for what he'd been craving all day; he
closed the distance between them, took her naked body in
his arms, and kissed her with all the force of his pent-up
desire. To his enormous relief, Devon kissed him back.

Nibbling at her lips, he muttered, "You're covered in
goosebumps. Come to bed, Devon."

"Just because I'm cold?"

"Because my heart's cold and I need you to warm it."

A muscle tightened in Jared's jaw. Where had those words come from? They weren't true, of course. Hyperbolic nonsense. It was just that she was so goddamned brave, walking into the kitchen without a stitch of clothing on.

Devon's smile went right through him. "Now that's a lot more persuasive than talk about goosebumps," she said. "I'd love to go to bed with you, Jared...if you're really sure you want to."

His blood had thickened in his veins with desire for her. "If...are you kidding?"

"You haven't touched me for days!"

"You're pregnant—I thought if we made love the way we did in New York I might hurt you," he said with at least partial truth, kissing her soundly between each phrase.

"Is that for real?" she demanded incredulously.

"Why else do you think I've been treating you like a nun?"

"Because you didn't want me any more! I'm the one who trapped you into marriage, remember?"

"Devon, it takes two people to make a baby. The first time we made love, birth control was the last thing on my mind...I'm just as responsible as you are." He cupped her buttocks in his hands, pressing her to his arousal. "I'll be gentle, I promise."

She shivered with longing. "Make love to me, Jared...oh, please, make love to me."

"Yes," he said. "Yes."

The first time, in the big bed with its window open to the velvet tropical night, Devon was aware of Jared holding back, treating her as though she were breakable china. The second time, with outright provocation, she seduced him into losing his control. As he shuddered to a climax in her arms, Devon held him close, his dark head against her breast. I love you, she thought in a burst of joy, and with inner shock, heard the words echo in her mind. Had she really fallen in love with her husband on the first night of their honeymoon?

She longed to say the words, to try them out on her tongue. Maybe that way she'd know if they were true. But an inner wisdom told her not to tell Jared. Not yet.

His heart was still hammering against her ribcage. She whispered, "Are you all right?"

"Yeah...you're like a wildcat, Devon." Then, without any pre-planning, the sentences fell from his lips. "That night in New York...yeah, it was a set-up to bring you down a peg or two. But once we were in bed, I forgot all about that—there was only the incredible intimacy of you and me together. It wasn't until morning, when I woke up, that I remembered I'd had a plan." His smile didn't reach his eyes. "And that was when I told you about it. As though it had been uppermost in my mind all night."

"Oh," said Devon. "Oh."

She was frowning. He added hoarsely, "Do you believe me?"

"Yes. Yes, I believe you."

He wanted to ask her if she forgave him. But the words wouldn't push themselves past the tightness in his throat. Very gently he stroked the slope of her shoulder, his arm brushing her breast, the contact rippling along his limbs.

"Thank you for telling me," Devon whispered.

When he looked up, her eyes were shining with unshed tears, and the soft curve of her mouth tightened his throat one more notch, touching him in a place so deep inside he hadn't known it existed. He said, not at all accurately, but he had to say something, "You look kind of like Turnip when he caught a mouse."

"There's not a romantic bone in your body," she said, her voice almost steady.

"So you're complaining already, Mrs. Holt?"

This time her smile was radiant. "No. Definitely not."

He laughed outright. "I've got a present for you."

"Another one?" she said saucily.

Still laughing, Jared got out of bed and crossed the room, unselfconscious in his nudity. Devon watched him, glorying in the smooth interplay of his muscles, the taut planes of his back and his ridged shoulderblades. She must love him. His body entranced her, along with everything he did to her with that body. And each time some small fraction of his feelings escaped him, he bound himself to her more tightly.

He came back holding a jeweler's box and held it out to her. He looked, she thought, uncharacteristically uncertain of himself. "I hope you like it," he said. "I know I'm doing this the wrong way round."

Slowly she opened the box. The ring was a star sapphire, gloriously blue, in an intricate antique setting. "Jared, it's beautiful," she breathed.

"You like it?"

She said shakily, "You could have bought me the biggest diamonds in the store. And you didn't. You bought me a ring you knew I'd love." Tears filled her eyes again, clinging to her lashes.

"Don't cry, Devon."

"I'm crying because I'm happy," she said. "But Jared, I didn't get you anything. I was scared to. Scared of the whole wedding scene."

He turned his wedding band on his finger. "The inscription about the third gift...what does that mean?"

She flushed. "The first one was me, I guess. When we made love at 'The Oaks.' The baby is the second gift."

Gifts without price, Jared thought, his mouth suddenly dry. Gifts that can't be bought, no matter how much money you have.

He didn't know how to say this in words. He'd said more than enough already. Instead he took her in his arms, inhaling the scent of her skin, so well known to him, so utterly familiar that he wondered how he'd ever lived without it. "Tomorrow," he said, "let's walk along the beach and make love under the stars."

"It's a plan," said Devon, and kissed him with such trust that there was a lump in Jared's chest.

He didn't know if the lump was emotion. It was a new sensation, one he'd never felt before with any other woman. A lump in his chest wasn't exactly the height of romance, either, he thought drily. But he knew he was exactly where he wanted to be, in bed with Devon curled up against him, her body relaxed, her breathing slowing to the rhythms of sleep.

Truly a priceless gift, was his last stray thought before he, too, fell asleep.

There was a crescent moon the following night, and a sky studded with stars that looked close enough for Devon to pluck them. Jared had wanted to go for a swim, but as she was feeling lazy she'd let him go alone, and half an hour later walked down to meet him at the beach. Going through the gate that had seemed so symbolic on her wedding day, she marveled at how different she felt from the woman who had wept in her white silk dress.

She didn't want to weep tonight. She wanted to sing and dance. Maybe, she thought, her cheeks flushing in the darkness, she'd dance naked for Jared on the beach. The sand was soft underfoot, and the low shoosh of the waves hypnotic. The water shone, starlight glinting on the foam.

She couldn't see Jared. She knew he was a strong swimmer who liked to exert himself, so at first she just wandered closer to the waves, the air warm on her skin. She could hear calypso music playing from the resort. Jared had said they might go there for dinner tomorrow. Her preference was to stay in the bungalow, eating the delicious meals that

Marisha, the housekeeper, left for them every day. She wasn't ready to be with other people yet.

She gazed out to sea, looking for Jared's dark head. The water was smooth and unbroken as far as she could see, the coral reef lying like a shadow pale as bone beneath the surface. With a twinge of unease, she looked closer, scanning the sea from left to right, then back again. His towel was still on the sand; she'd passed it on her way here.

Jared wouldn't have gone back to the bungalow without his towel; anyway, she'd have seen him.

He'd been stung by a ray. He'd had a cramp and drowned. He'd been a victim of a shark attack. All the dangers of the sea rushed through her mind, and with a moan of terror she raked the sea again with her eyes, straining to see him in the darkness.

Nothing. Devon shouted his name, running along the edge of the sea, the waves splashing her ankles. She knew there was no point in swimming around trying to find him. She'd be better to get help.

Frantically she looked around. Among the tall palms a light shone. Marisha's house. Marisha would know what to do. Devon started to run, and as she ran the truth seared its way through her brain. Of course she loved Jared. Loved him with all her heart, and always would. She couldn't lose him; such a loss would be unbearable.

As she reached the palms and the shrubs of sea grape, stones dug into her soles. She kept running, the light closer now, her eyes trained on the path. Then, as she rounded a corner, a dark figure detached itself from the shrubs, looming over her. Devon screamed and stopped dead.

"Devon?" Jared said. His voice sharpened. "Are you hurt?"

Jared. Jared standing in the middle of the path. Not drowned. Not devoured by sharks. Devon swayed, her head whirling, and felt him take her by the waist and lower her to the path, pushing her head between her legs. "Take a couple of slow breaths," he ordered.

Gradually the world righted itself. "When I went down to the beach, your towel was there, but not you." Her breath caught on a sob. "I thought you'd drowned. Or sharks had got you."

"I met up with David—Marisha's husband—and he wanted to show me the conch he got today. I didn't realize you were coming down to meet me."

She grabbed him by the arm, holding on as hard as she could. "I was s-so frightened. I couldn't bear it if anything happened to you."

"Devon..." he said in an odd voice.

Finally she looked up. His expression was unreadable; in her bones she knew he'd retreated to a place where she couldn't reach him, and her impulse to tell him she loved him died stillborn. He thought she was being over-emotional. Hysterical. "I—I'm sorry," she faltered. "I guess I overreacted."

"I didn't mean to frighten you," he said flatly. "I'm not used to people fussing over me."

"I wasn't fussing! I was worried sick."

"Okay, okay...I'm not used to that, either."

"Are you angry?" she asked in a small voice.

"No." He moved his shoulders restlessly. "Let's go home."

Home was the bungalow where she'd known such happiness. Home was where Jared was. "All right...I was going to dance for you, naked, on the beach. But now you'll have to wait until tomorrow."

"You were?" Pulling her to her feet, he suddenly grinned at her in the darkness, his teeth very white. "You know what? I like you, Devon—I like the way I never know what you're going to do next. I'm beginning to think my life was entirely too predictable before I met you."

It wasn't exactly a declaration of passionate love. But coming from Jared, who so rarely spoke of his feelings, it meant a lot. As they walked back to the bungalow hand in hand, Devon was aware of how happy she was. A honeymoon, she thought, was a marvellous invention. Especially when it was spent with Jared.

Over the next three days Jared and Devon made love on the beach under the crescent moon after Devon danced naked for him; they made love against the kitchen door and in the Jacuzzi and in the pool; they even made love in bed. Devon sang in the shower, and filled the bungalow with flowers. Not even the fact that Jared spent a couple of hours every morning closeted with his computer and fax machine bothered her. During those times she went for walks along the beach, watching the frigate birds dive, and picking up shells from the white sand. She was happy. So happy, so deeply in love with her husband, that she was filled with optimism.

Jared had shown her such tenderness and depths of passion the last few days that she couldn't believe he wouldn't fall in love with her. Perhaps, she thought, admiring the blazing orange flowers of the tulip tree by their bungalow, he already had.

Liking was a big step toward love, wasn't it?

In her short yellow sundress, magenta bougainvillea woven into her hair, she went back into the bungalow. Jared was still on the phone. She went into the kitchen to make some papaya juice. She adored papayas.

Tomorrow they were to fly to Vancouver. While she hated to leave the island where she'd been so happy, Jared was going to Vancouver with her and staying for a few days. An extended honeymoon, she thought with a quiver of anticipation, and found herself smiling idiotically at the refrigerator door.

She'd never realized how wonderful it was to be in love.

Still smiling, she took a glass of juice to the little study that was off the living room and tapped on the door. Jared was on the phone. Opening the door, she put the juice on the table beside him. He was barking instructions into the mouthpiece, jabbing at his notepad with a pencil, and didn't even glance at her.

It was the other side to Jared: the businessman, efficient and ruthless. Quickly she went out again, and started making a salad for lunch. Half an hour later Jared joined her. He said abruptly, "Devon, I'll take you to the house tomorrow. But I won't be able to stay. I'll have to go to Singapore right away, and I'm not sure how long I'll be gone."

Her disappointment was crushing. Trying hard not to let it show, she said, "Could I go with you? I don't have to be in London for the conferences until the following week."

"I never mix business and pleasure—I told you that."

He sounded so detached he could have been talking about interest rates or the composite index. "I'm your wife," she said steadily. "Surely that's a little different?"

He said impatiently, "Look, I can be with you in Vancouver tomorrow afternoon and see you settled in. But I'll have to get the overnight flight out."

Devon fought to sound reasonable and mature, even though she felt neither one. "What's going on in Singapore?"

"It's too complicated to explain," he said with some of the same impatience.

"Try me."

She watched him gulp down the juice, the muscles in his throat moving as he swallowed. Last night she'd lain her cheek against his throat, her breasts warm to his ribcage...

"I've got a couple more hours on the phone yet," he said. "Call me when lunch is ready."

"Jared, I'm a smart woman—I'm sure I'm capable of understanding a crisis in Singapore. Or anywhere else for that matter."

"I don't have the time!"

Again she strove for patience. "Then give me a kiss before you go."

He said curtly, "If I do that, you know where we'll end up."

"Kissing isn't just about sex," Devon blurted, and knew she'd stumbled on an important truth.

"With you and me it is."

He probably meant the words as a compliment. Feeling cold inside, Devon faltered, "What about affection...and caring?"

With an irritated shrug, he said, "Why do women always have to drag in emotion, no matter what the issue?"

"I'm not some sort of generic woman—I'm your wife. And emotions are all-important."

"For Pete's sake, Devon, there's a time and place for everything... If there's any of that conch salad left, I'd like it for lunch."

Then he was gone. Devon sat down hard on the nearest stool. Barefoot and pregnant in the kitchen, ladling out salad. Or sexy in bed. Was that really how Jared saw her? Two different stereotypes, and neither one a real woman, with feelings.

He wasn't in love with her; she'd been deceiving herself to even consider the possibility. She turned him on, no doubt of that. But he wasn't going to let her invade the rest of his life. To truly become his wife and share all the things that were important to him: the world of business and sudden crises and board meetings. No, that wasn't part of his plan.

She was a fringe benefit, she thought numbly. Beautiful, passionate, nice to have around for the honeymoon. But after that relegated to her proper place.

Turned off like a switch. The way he'd kissed her hand, at Benson and Alicia's wedding.

Covering her ears, Devon tried to blot out the sound of Jared's voice on the phone. She'd been a fool to fall in love with him. A silly fool. Because once he tired of her sexually, what would they have left? Absolutely nothing.

At three o'clock the next afternoon Devon was crossing another threshold, that of an imposing mansion that overlooked a golf course, the gray waters of the bay, and the sharp peaks of the Rocky Mountains, silhouetted against roiling, dark-edged clouds. The staff had seen to it that the house was warm and immaculately clean, but it would take a lot more than a good housekeeper to infuse it with welcome, Devon thought, looking around her as she trailed from room to room.

Architecturally, the house made the most of its panoramic view; but the furniture was austere, the colors neutral, and the overall effect was of a perfect setting for entertaining important people. It wasn't a home. To be lived in. By a husband, his wife, and their baby.

Jared was on the phone again, checking his reservations. The magic of their honeymoon had been flawed for Devon ever since that brief conversation in the kitchen of the bungalow; while she'd been quite unable to resist the passion of his caresses last night, the soul had gone from it. It was lovemaking only as far as she was concerned. Not for him.

Then Jared spoke from behind her. "You'll be fine here, Devon. The housekeeper and groundsman live in the cottage by the road, their names are Sally and Thomas, and the security system's top of the line. There's a car for your use in the garage, Thomas has all the keys and can show you around.''

"It feels empty," she said.

"Well, it has been. For nearly two years." He gave her a preoccupied smile. "Let's go out for dinner. Then I'll have to head to the airport."

She didn't ask to go to airport with him. What was the use? Feeling the first kindlings of anger that Jared could dump her in a house with as much soul as a magazine showplace, then take off without her for an unspecified length of time, Devon said coldly, "I'm not very hungry."

"You've got to eat."

"For the sake of the baby." He nodded. "Jared," Devon said, "do you love me?"

His face froze to stillness. "Why do you ask?"

Wishing she hadn't asked, she said steadily, "Because I want to know the answer."

"I told you once before that I'm not capable of falling in love."

Now that she'd started, Devon couldn't stop. "So what do you feel toward me?"

"I care about you," he said tersely, looking about as uncaring as a man could look. "What's the matter—didn't you enjoy our honeymoon, Devon?"

"I loved it. But now it's over. Where do we go from here? That's what I want to know."

"I have no idea."

His voice was as unfeeling as a recording, and the man himself as impervious as granite. She should never have started this, Devon thought with a chill of despair. It was useless to fight him: she should have remembered that. "Why don't you grab something to eat at the airport?" she said evenly. "I'm tired and jet-lagged. I think I'll lie down for a while."

Lie down with me. That was what she wanted him to do.

His arms around her, holding her in this cold, imposing house, somehow making it, even minimally, their own. But she was too proud to beg him to take her in his arms, and too stubborn to cry in front of him. She'd done that once. She wasn't going to do it again.

"Maybe that's what I'll do. I'm all packed, and I could get Gregson to meet me at the airport so we could go over some figures."

Devon had no idea who Gregson was. She didn't ask. "I hope everything will go well," she said, as politely as if he were a distant cousin, and not the man whose body had brought her such fulfillment and felicity. Such joy.

Jared was frowning. "Take care of yourself, Devon...you do look tired. Thomas will drive me to the airport, and I'll call you tomorrow."

He kissed her quickly on the cheek, and walked out of the room. Devon wandered into the library, whose windows overlooked the driveway with its formal arrangements of shrubbery. She loathed topiary. A car pulled up, a gray-haired man got out and helped Jared with his luggage, and then the two of them drove away. The car was a black Mercedes. Nothing but the best, Devon thought, and stared out over the windswept waters of the bay.

CHAPTER ELEVEN

DEVON tried very hard to like the house. On Jared's first phone call—he was punctilious about keeping in touch—he gave her carte blanche to spend whatever she liked on it. She redecorated the sunroom; only after she'd finished did she realize that unwittingly she'd done her best to fill the room with the atmosphere of the bungalow on the little tropical island where she'd been so happy. After that, there didn't seem to be much sense in changing anything else. This wasn't the bungalow. And she wasn't happy.

She almost wished Jared didn't phone so promptly every day. He sounded miles away, both in terms of actual distance as well as emotionally. Slowly and painfully she was coming to the conclusion she'd been fooling herself that his emotions were buried and that she'd be able to unearth them. They weren't buried. He didn't have any feelings. Not for her, anyway.

He was delayed in the Far East. He'd been gone two weeks when Patrick phoned her; Patrick had a four-hour stopover in Vancouver, on his way north. Devon drove out to meet him, and they had a very enjoyable lunch together. Patrick was fun. They talked the same language, Devon thought; Patrick didn't shut her out, like Jared. And while she was tempted to tell Patrick how unhappy she was, she didn't do so. Her primary loyalty, she knew, lay with Jared.

The next day Devon flew to London for the last two conferences on her contract, and after that to Baffin Island, her final commitment before she was officially on leave. Her flight from Iqaluit back to Montreal was delayed three successive times due to blizzards; when she did get off the plane, she was dazed with tiredness.

She walked in the direction of the baggage signs; she had an overnight stay in the city before heading back to Vancouver. She should go and see Benson and Alicia, now that she was this close. But she didn't want to. How could she act like a happy newly-wed when she wasn't? She wouldn't be able to deceive either one of them. No, she was better off staying away from "The Oaks."

In the baggage area, Devon checked which carousel was for her flight. A man was waiting underneath the sign, a tall, black-haired man who stood out from the crowd. Her heart turned over in her breast, then beat a staccato against her ribs. He was wearing a trench coat over his business suit; his eyes had flown to her face. Which felt as stiff as a board.

She hadn't seen Jared for well over three weeks. She said sharply, "Alicia and Benson—there's nothing wrong, is there?"

He shook his head. "Let's get your bags."

"Why are you here?"

"I heard about your flight delays. I was on my way to New York, so I made a detour."

"That doesn't answer my question," she said tautly.

"I've booked us into a hotel. We'll talk there."

You're damn right we will, she thought militantly, and sneaked a glance at his unyielding profile. It wasn't fair that he was so big, so overpoweringly masculine, so undeniably sexy. She didn't feel one bit sexy. She felt like a woman who was four and a half months pregnant and needed to put her feet up.

Three-quarters of an hour later, Jared ushered her into a suite in Montreal's most expensive hotel. It reminded her so strongly of the house in Vancouver, perfectly decorated and soulless, that she was suddenly desperately homesick for her condo, for her life before she met Jared.

He said brusquely, "What are you thinking about?"

"Nothing."

"Devon, you look wiped. You've got to take better care of yourself...I know you're past the miscarriage stage, but you shouldn't be overextending yourself like this."

"Go to hell, Jared," she said with the calm of extreme rage.

"What kind of an answer's that? Look at you—circles under your eyes, and if you don't sit down soon, you're going to pass out."

She glared at him. "All you care about is the baby!"

"Don't you?" he grated.

It was the cruelest thing he could have said. She said tightly, "I've been in these clothes for the last two days— I'm going to have a bath. Order something light for supper, will you?" Then she marched into the bathroom and slammed the door.

He hadn't denied that the baby was all he cared about.

Wearily Devon turned on the bath, washing her hair first, then soaking in the hot water. She shouldn't have lost her temper, she thought, making little ripples with her fingers. It hadn't helped matters at all. She wouldn't lose it again. She'd be rational and calm and detached. As unemotional as Jared.

She got out, wrapped herself in a huge bath towel, and turned on the drier for her hair. A few minutes later Jared knocked on the door. "Devon? May I come in?"

For a moment she hesitated. Then she called in a clear voice, "Of course."

Jared walked in. She was sitting in front of the mirror, the towel around her hips, brushing her hair. It shone like silk. Her breasts were fuller, he thought, dry-mouthed, her skin had the ivory sheen that he found so heart-stoppingly beautiful. Then he saw the slightly rounded swell of her belly where the child—his child, their child—was growing. He walked over to her, dropped to his haunches, and laid his hand on her smooth skin. He said huskily, "You're starting to show, Devon."

"It's over four months. Halfway now."

He said in a taut voice, "I'm not just worrying about the baby—I was worried about you, too. Stuck up there miles from medical help in the middle of a blizzard—I was nearly out of my mind."

"I shouldn't have lost my temper."

He gave her a faint smile. "You wouldn't be you if you hadn't." Then, in a gesture that melted her heart, Jared laid his cheek against her belly.

She stroked his hair, closing her eyes, and felt him reach up to caress her breasts. "Let's go to bed," he whispered. "It's the only place I can show you what you mean to me."

"Yes," she murmured, "take me to bed, Jared." And did her best to ignore the fleeting thought that she and Jared couldn't spend their entire married life in bed.

What if that was the only place she meant anything to him?

The next morning, eating strawberries that had come with their breakfast, Devon said, "Let me come to New York with you, Jared. I can stay at your place, do some Christmas shopping."

A trickle of juice had gathered at the corner of her mouth. Jared reached over with his serviette and wiped it away. "I'll only be there one night," he said. "Then I'm off to Texas for a board meeting."

"I could stay in the penthouse until you come back."

"Devon, we decided to make our home in Vancouver. And I don't want you doing any more flying than necessary."

"I'm not ill! I'm pregnant. Anyway, the house in Vancouver doesn't feel like a home."

He tried hard to hold onto his patience. "I know I haven't been there much, but—"

"You haven't been there at all."

"With the money markets the way they are, I've been busier than usual...once things settle down, I'll be able to spend more time with you."

She swallowed her pride. "I'm lonely there, Jared."

"I'll phone a couple of contacts I have out there, and see that you get into the social swim."

Her chin jerked up. "You will not! If you can't be bothered to introduce me to your friends yourself, I'll do without."

He said coldly, "You're being illogical. You say you're lonely, but you turn your back on my offer of help."

Again Devon strove for the exact truth. "It's you I'm lonely for, Jared. Not your friends."

"Devon, I work hard—the sooner you learn that, the better. I travel a lot. I have to. And I won't have you tagging along, not when you're pregnant."

"The result of pregnancy is a child," she said with deadly calm. "You won't want a child bothering you when your mind's on business any more than you want me bothering you now."

Jared tore a piece of toast in half and grabbed the butter knife. There wasn't a business opponent he'd ever come across who could knock him off balance: he'd always managed to stay two steps ahead of the competition. So how could a blond-haired woman make him feel so beleaguered? So much in the wrong? Guilty, for Pete's sake? "I'm making sure our child's inheritance is in good shape," he said coldly.

"Maybe it's better for a child to have a father than an

inheritance,'' she retorted. ''Even if you can't be bothered to be home for the mother.''

''One of the reasons I've been so successful is that I've never allowed myself to be distracted from business matters—and I'm not going to start now.''

Filled with the same sense of impotence she'd had before she married Jared, the same conviction that it was hopeless to oppose him, Devon said, ''Fine. You do as you please. I'll have dinner with Patrick in Toronto tonight, and then I'm going to 'The Oaks' for a visit.''

''Patrick?'' he rapped.

''Your cousin,'' she said with overdone patience.

''I know who he is. How do you know he's in Toronto?''

''He faxed me in London.''

''So you're in regular contact with him?'' Jared demanded through gritted teeth and a jealousy bitter as lye.

''Of course not. We had lunch together once at the Vancouver airport while you were in the Far East—that's the only time I've seen him since your father's birthday. But I like Patrick. He's fun.''

''The implication being that I'm not?''

''I didn't say so, Jared!''

He strove to push down the turmoil in his chest. The thought of Devon with another man made him feel physically ill: a sensation he hated. What had happened to his control, his almost superhuman ability to keep his life compartmentalized—business here, pleasure there? Shot to hell, he thought grimly. Ever since he'd taken into his bed a tall woman with blond hair and eyes blue as the sea. A woman whose beauty made nonsense of his rules.

Dammit, those rules had served him well. He wasn't going to give them up for anyone. Not even Devon. He said shortly, ''Lunch at an airport isn't the same thing as dinner in Toronto. Where will you stay?''

''If you don't trust me,'' she seethed, ''you can always hire another private investigator.''

Didn't he trust her? Was that what this was all about?

Jared hesitated too long, and saw the anger in her face eclipsed by pain. A pain she hid almost immediately, but which filled him with an obscure rage. ''Of course I trust you,'' he said.

''It doesn't sound to me as though you do.'' Devon stood up, her face very pale. ''I can't take any more of this—you win again, Jared. I'll get a direct flight to Vancouver, and you can let me know when you'll be back... Excuse me, I'm going to call the airline.''

She went into their bedroom and closed the door. Jared ate a mouthful of toast, which could have been a floppy disc for all the taste it had, and tried to make himself concentrate on his strategy for the board meeting in Texas.

Devon had been back in Vancouver for four days when she had a visitor. She'd flown direct from Montreal, telling Benson and Alicia that she wasn't feeling well and needed to get home. She and Jared had parted with a civility that had covered, at least on her part, a maelstrom of anger, hurt and love. Falling in love, she was concluding, was the stupidest move of her entire life.

Which didn't make her fall out of love. She didn't know how to do that.

She wasn't sure it was possible.

The sunroom was misnamed, because rainy day followed rainy day, the skies as gray as her mood. Nevertheless, Devon spent a lot of her time there, for it was the only place in the house that bore her stamp. Moving her computer to a desk that overlooked the garden, she wrote her reports for the conferences she'd attended and for the Arctic trip, and started making plans to brush up on her German and French after Christmas. She was rather looking forward to less traveling; the stress of her job had been beginning to get to her for the last year or so.

She was in the sunroom watering the plants when Sally appeared at the door. Devon was doing her best to like Sally, although she found her both dour and unapproachable. Sally said, "Someone to see you, Mrs. Holt. Her name is Lise Lamont."

Water splashed from the can onto the tile floor. Devon bent to wipe it up, her heart thumping uncomfortably fast. Why would Lise come to see her? Wishing she wasn't wearing sweatpants and a baggy sweater, she said coolly, "Show her in, please, Sally. And perhaps you could bring us some coffee?"

Straightening, she ran her fingers through her hair and did her best to look composed. Sally ushered Lise in and disappeared to get the coffee. Devon said pleasantly, "How nice to see you, Lise...and how well you look."

Lise was wearing a designer label pantsuit in navy wool, with a vivid scarlet sweater; her makeup was impeccable. "I'm glad I caught you home," she said with a smile that barely moved her lips. "Jared told me you were here."

Doing her best to ignore this piece of information, Devon said, "Do sit down...Sally will bring us some coffee. Isn't the weather awful?"

For the five minutes it took for Sally to reappear, they talked about the rain, Chinatown, and the ski runs at Whistler. Then Devon poured the coffee and offered Lise a plate of almond cookies. Lise took one, saying, "I hear you're pregnant."

"Yes. I'm feeling very well...morning sickness was no joke, though."

"When are you due?"

"Late spring."

"Clever of you."

So the gloves were off, thought Devon. "Clever? I'm not sure I follow you."

"Clever of you to trap Jared into marriage. You weren't the first to try, of course—but you were the first to succeed." Delicately Lise sipped her coffee. "I made the mistake of underestimating you at the wedding. Jared always has an eye for a pretty girl...but I didn't think anything would come of it. It never has in the past."

"Perhaps, Lise, you should ask Jared whether it was he or I who insisted we get married. The answer might surprise you."

Lise's pale blue eyes narrowed, and momentarily she looked far from beautiful. "I already know the answer. You refused to have an abortion. Jared chose not to father a bastard child who'd attract the attention of the gutter press. He's a proud man. Of course he married you."

Carefully Devon put her bone china cup back on its saucer, watching the reflections move in the tall glass windows: two women drinking coffee in a room she'd done her best to make homelike. An outsider might have thought the women were friends, but such a picture was false. Lise was an enemy. "He'll never divorce me," Devon said.

"When you see what I've brought, you might want to divorce him," Lise said, and reached down for her snakeskin bag.

Devon's nerves tightened. They'd come to the real reason for Lise's visit, she thought. All the rest had been the lead-in. Setting the stage. And she herself one of the actresses, the one who didn't know her lines because she'd never read the play.

Lise pulled an envelope from her handbag. "A couple of these photos were taken in Singapore a short while ago," she said. "The rest are at Jared's penthouse—I expect you'll recognize it."

Devon was proud to see that her fingers were steady as

she took the envelope and extracted the small pile of photos. The first depicted a crowded street along an inlet packed with sampans, all with colorful awnings. Jared was smiling down at the woman walking by his side: Lise, looking petite and elegant in a sleeveless green dress. In another shot they were posed outside Raffles Hotel. The other photos were all taken in Manhattan: Lise and Jared dancing in a disco, laughing at each other amidst a gathering of people in Jared's living room, arm in arm on the street near Central Park. In each of the photos the intimacy between the couple hurt Devon deep inside. She said sharply, "These could have been taken any time. You've known Jared quite a while."

"Why do you think he didn't want you going to Singapore with him?" Lise murmured. As Devon's face changed, Lise laughed softly. "I would have gone to Texas with him, too, but I thought it more important I come out here instead. Surely it's better for you to find out the truth now, rather than later."

"How altruistic of you," Devon replied, trying to stuff the photos back in the envelope. One of them fell to the floor: Lise in a stunning sequined dress, caught in Jared's arms as they danced. Devon scrabbled for it clumsily, and without meeting Lise's eyes put the envelope on the coffee table. Desperately wanting the other woman to be gone so she could be alone, she said, "If you think Jared will divorce me and marry you, you're quite wrong. First of all, one of the conditions of our marriage was that there be no divorce. Secondly, he had his chance to marry you…and he didn't take it, did he?"

Lise flushed, her lips narrowing. "Jared made a very foolish mistake in marrying you. He's already realizing that."

"He hasn't said so to me."

"He certainly has to me. If you have any sense, Devon,

any dignity, you'll disappear from his life. Out of sight is most certainly out of mind as far as Jared's concerned.''

''In that case, you'd better get back to Manhattan, hadn't you?'' Devon said, getting to her feet as regally as if she also were wearing a designer label suit rather than pale pink sweatpants and a sweater with bunny rabbits embroidered on the collar.

Lise stood up, too. She looked furious, Devon saw with distant satisfaction. ''I can see myself out,'' Lise snapped. ''Don't try and hang onto Jared, Devon—he doesn't want you.''

''It was me he took to bed after my mother's wedding and Benson's birthday dinner—not you,'' Devon said. ''Goodbye, Lise.''

Lise's heels tapped sharply down the oak flooring. She shut the front door with noticeable force. Slowly Devon sat down, and only then noticed that Lise had left the photos on the coffee table. She looked at them again, one by one, and all she could think was how Jared had refused to take her to Singapore, and how he hadn't wanted her to go to Manhattan with him, or to Texas.

For business reasons. That was what he'd said.

With a whimper of pain, she hunched forward. He'd taken Lise to Singapore instead. And Lise lived in Manhattan; she was always available there. Especially with Devon four thousand miles away.

Devon's only stipulation when Jared had urged marriage had been that he be faithful to her. It was just over a month since the wedding, and it seemed already he'd broken his word. Remembering how readily he'd agreed to that stipulation, she now realized he'd never meant to abide by it. He'd lied to her from the start; he couldn't be trusted.

She'd known that, ever since the night in New York. So why had she taken him at his word and assumed that he and Lise were no longer lovers? And why had she fallen in love with him?

What a fool she'd been!

Devon got up eventually, afraid that Sally would come in and find her weeping into her empty coffee cup. As she wiped her face in the bathroom off the master bedroom, her initial impulse was to book the first flight to New York and confront Jared. But what was the use? If it was Lise he wanted, she, Devon, couldn't alter that by yelling at him. Or by sobbing her heart out.

Anyway, Jared was in Texas, and the sooner she accepted she'd been a temporary diversion in his life, the better.

Steve. Peter. And now Jared.

She pulled on a jacket and went for a walk along the seafront. When she came back, there was a message from Jared on the answering machine in her bedroom. In the deep baritone so achingly familiar to her, he said he was flying to San Francisco and would arrive in Vancouver by the end of the week; Thomas could meet him at the airport. He could have been talking to Thomas or Sally, Devon thought, for all the emotion in his voice.

She sat down on the edge of the bed. She wasn't going to cry; there'd be time for that later. What she had to do was come up with a plan of action.

She was going to take Lise's advice. She was going to disappear from Jared's life.

Even though she wasn't at all convinced Jared would try to trace her, by the next morning Devon had decided to cover her tracks. He'd had her investigated once; what was there stopping him from trailing her this time? So her first step was to give Thomas and Sally two weeks' leave. Blushing from her duplicity, hoping they'd think she was blushing from embarrassment, she said, "Jared and I have had so little time together, we'd rather like the place to ourselves for a few days... I can arrange bookings for you, if you'd like to go somewhere.''

Sally smiled, for once looking quite human. ''We could go and see our grandchildren in Calgary, couldn't we, Tom?''

''You're sure about this, Mrs. Holt? Mr. Holt didn't mention it to me,'' Thomas said doubtfully.

''I'll take full responsibility,'' Devon said. ''Let me book your tickets for tomorrow.''

By noon the following day the Holts were gone. In the empty house, Devon wrote a letter to Jared and phoned a courier to pick it up. Her final revision was brief.

Jared,

Lise came to see me, bringing the photos I'm enclosing with this letter. They're self-explanatory; I understand now why you didn't want me to go to Singapore with you, or even to Manhattan. I only wish you'd told me the truth.

I'm leaving you, Jared. You see, I did something very silly on our honeymoon—I fell in love with you. In consequence, I can't bear to share you with another woman.

Please don't come after me or try to find me.

She signed it simply ''Devon,'' and addressed it to his penthouse. She also wrote to Benson and Alicia, telling them that she was going away for a while, and they weren't to worry. This letter she decided to send by ordinary mail. After the courier came, she called a cab.

The taxi took Devon to the train station, where she changed her clothes in the women's washroom and emerged looking very different. She took another cab to within a block of the bus station and caught a bus that took her onto the Vancouver Island ferry. She spoke to no one during the crossing, and once the bus reached Victoria she found a charming bed and breakfast by the waterfront that would take cash; she registered under an assumed name. All these precautions felt at one and the same time both ludicrous and absolutely necessary.

Her room was very private, down a little corridor. Devon locked the door and lay down on the bed. All day she'd been fighting back tears. But now that she was alone, the tears wouldn't come. Her eyes burning, she stared into the darkness, feeling more alone than she had ever felt.

Jared had been unfaithful to her. Jared didn't love her.

Jared was chairing the board meeting in Austin when his secretary brought him a message. "Excuse me, gentlemen," he said, swiveled his chair round, and unfolded the paper. It must be important; his secretary knew better than to interrupt for anything trivial.

His valet in Manhattan had phoned. A letter had been delivered by courier from Mrs. Holt in Vancouver. The valet awaited Mr. Holt's instructions.

Jared stared at the paper, reading it again, aware of tension tightening his shoulderblades. Why would Devon send a message by courier? She had only to phone if something was wrong.

The baby. Had something happened to the baby? But a courier message? It made no sense. He pushed back his chair. "I'll be right back," he said, and left the room.

Wallace, his valet, answered the phone on the second ring. "Holt residence. May I help you?"

Wallace Henty had worked for Benson when Jared was in his teens; Jared trusted his discretion implicitly. "Wallace, will you open the letter from Mrs. Holt, please, and read it to me?"

"Certainly, sir."

Jared could hear the sound of cardboard tearing. Then

Wallace said noncommittally, "The package includes a number of photographs, sir. Of you and Miss Lamont."

Jared's hand clenched around the receiver. "What photos?"

"Looks like Singapore to me, sir. Three more taken here, and a couple at Giorgio's disco."

Jared said tightly, "Is there a letter?"

"Yes, sir." Sounding as placid as if he were perusing the phone book, Wallace read Devon's letter.

In a cracked voice, Jared said, "Read it again." But the words were exactly the same the second time. Devon was convinced he was having an affair with Lise. Devon loved him. Devon had left him and didn't want him coming after her. He said urgently, "Have there been any other messages from Mrs. Holt?"

"No, sir."

"If there are, you're to get in touch with me immediately. Have you got that? Immediately." Then Jared rang off. He dialed the house in Vancouver, letting the phone ring a dozen times before he cut the connection, nor did he get any response from either Sally or Thomas at the cottage. Where the devil was everyone?

He phoned Alicia and Benson next. "Alicia, it's Jared. Is Devon there?"

"No...she's in Vancouver, isn't she?"

It was too late for either tact or discretion. "She's left me. I don't know where she is. I'd hoped she'd have been in touch with you."

"*Left* you?"

"Yes. She thought I was having an affair with Lise."

Even as he spoke the words Jared knew that part of his inner tumult was hurt that Devon hadn't trusted him. But then he, more than most, should know what a convincing actress Lise could be. Put that together with the evidence of the photos, and it was a damning scenario. He wasn't quite prepared to admit that his own behavior the last few weeks could have had something to do with it, too.

"Are you having an affair?" Alicia demanded.

She sounded as fierce as any mother protecting her young. "No, I'm not," he said roundly. "I've never slept with Lise and I never will. I'm going to try and trace Devon, Alicia. And for God's sake, if you or Dad hear from her, let me know, will you? Wallace always knows where I can be reached."

Alicia said, "Jared, do you love my daughter?"

"I don't know!" he said, exasperated.

"I think it's about time you figured it out. Devon's been hurt by men before. She doesn't need you toying with her affections."

Toying with her affections? What was that supposed to mean? "I'll do my best," he said sarcastically.

"High time," Alicia announced. "All women aren't like Beatrice or Lise. Or even like me in my let's-get-married-and-have-a-nice-divorce days. Devon can be proud and stubborn. But she can also be very loving."

"She fell in love with me on our honeymoon," Jared heard himself say, and scowled into the receiver. He'd had no intention of sharing that piece of information with anyone. Not until he'd had the time to think about it. Digest it.

"Don't you dare break my daughter's heart, Jared Holt," Alicia said. Then she put the phone down in his ear.

Women, he thought savagely, and dialed Information. In the next few minutes he talked to Sally and Thomas at their son's place in Calgary, and ordered his private investigation firm to get on Devon's trail. Then he put down the phone.

Now what? The board meeting was far from finished, and the most important item of business had been left to the end. Briskly Jared walked back into the boardroom.

CHAPTER TWELVE

DEVON must have resolved something during the long hours she'd spent gazing at the ceiling's gray rectangle in her room in Victoria. The next day, after breakfast, she went for a walk, deliberately trying to calm her mind. She had the baby to think of. She couldn't afford to get run down or overly emotional. She must forget about the past, about Jared, and think only of the future. Perhaps she'd settle in this charming old-world city for the next few months. There'd be lots of opportunities to do translation work here.

She bought a couple of novels; she went to a matinee of a movie she'd wanted to see; she ate supper in a vegetarian restaurant, reading one of the novels. Then she took a cab back to her room.

There were, of course, no messages.

She closed the door to her room, spreading her purchases around to make the room look more lived in. Jared, she thought in sudden desperation, oh, Jared, how could you?

Her storm of weeping was brief. She dried her eyes and got ready for bed. And this time it wasn't loneliness that was her bedfellow, but desire. All she wanted in the world, she thought in despair, was what she couldn't have: Jared beside her, his mouth on hers, his hands on her body. Jared faithful to her because he loved her.

She might as well ask for the moon.

The next day Devon had afternoon tea at The Empress Hotel, a ceremony that was an institution in Victoria. Her table was close to that of two other women, who were dissecting the marital difficulties of a number of their

169

friends. Devon listened with half an ear, trying to find it funny that she wasn't alone in her misery: adultery, it seemed, was rampant. Adultery was an odd word, she mused; there was nothing very adult about it.

Then her attention sharpened. "If I had to choose," the younger woman was saying, the one wearing a beaded turban, "I'd take Derek any day. He doesn't say much, but he's kind of solid. You can trust him. Harold, now—oh, Harold's charming, cute as all get out, but I wouldn't take one word he says to the bank. No way. Go for Derek, Marcy."

Devon sat frozen, a petit four halfway to her mouth, which was open. Harold sounded like Lise, charming, decorative, and out for number one. Whereas Jared—he didn't say much, just like Derek. But when he did try and talk about his feelings, he was doing his best to tell the truth.

One by one the pictures flashed through Devon's brain. Jared telling her about Beatrice and Turnip, the ugly orange tomcat whom he'd loved. Jared's face when he'd covered her with his big body in bed at the bungalow, the tenderness in his eyes the night they'd made love on the beach. Even his anger when he'd railed to her about business, his jealousy when she'd mentioned the dinner with Patrick. All there. Above board. Out in the open.

Yet Devon had put her trust in Lise. Not in Jared.

"Is everything all right, madam?"

Devon put the cake down and gave the waitress a bemused look. "Yes," she said. "Yes, it is. In fact, it's getting better by the minute."

She'd been a fool. She'd taken the photos at face value. She'd allowed Lise—a famous Broadway actress—to drive her away from her own husband. To send her into hiding and cut herself off from the man she loved.

She was going back to Vancouver. As fast as she could. And then she was going to find Jared, and tell him face to face that she loved him and was willing to wait for however long it took for him to fall in love with her.

He would fall in love with her eventually... wouldn't he?

It was dark when Devon got back. The house looked deserted and unfriendly. The trees had long ago lost their leaves, their branches bony against the sky. Frost had killed the last of the flowers, and Thomas, of course, was away instead of being here to clean them up. She paid off the cabbie and went inside, very aware of all the empty rooms, of her footsteps echoing on the parquet floor.

At the door of the sunroom, she stopped and looked around uneasily. She hadn't left the phone book out like that, had she? And her papers had been neatly piled on the desk, not scattered all over it.

Her heart fluttering like a trapped bird, she went upstairs to the master bedroom. Drawers had been pulled out, her closet door gaped open, and someone had sat on the bed. Jared? It had to be Jared. Otherwise the security system would have alerted the police.

But he wasn't here now. No suitcase, no other signs of occupancy, not even in the kitchen, which was just as she'd left it. If he'd been here, he'd gone again.

He hadn't bothered leaving a note.

Briefly Devon contemplated spending the night in a hotel. But the thought of the phone calls to get a reservation, and of making another journey, defeated her. She'd be fine here.

She went downstairs, staring dubiously at the panel of the security system. She was pretty sure it was set right. She didn't want to start playing about with it, because if she did something wrong and set it off the police would come roaring up the driveway.

She didn't need that.

Switching off all the lights, she trailed upstairs, discovering within herself a strong dislike of sleeping all alone in the kingsized bed in the master bedroom. She'd done that while Sally was here; Sally wouldn't have approved the mistress of the house using one of the guest bedrooms. But Sally was in Calgary. She, Devon, could do as she pleased. She pushed open the door of the smallest of the guest rooms, with its bay window that overlooked the woods, and its attractive brick fireplace. She'd sleep here. Maybe then she wouldn't feel so lonely.

Devon put her case on the bed and picked up the phone. Chewing on her lip, she dialed Jared's penthouse, desperate for him to answer, longing for his deep baritone to calm all her fears across the many miles that separated them. But on the fourth ring, the answering machine clicked in. "Jared," she said tremulously, "it's Devon. I'm back in Vancouver. Will you phone me as soon as possible, please?" She took a deep breath. "I love you." Then she put down the receiver.

He should be home now, shouldn't he? In between his trips to Texas and San Francisco?

Maybe he was out with Lise.

She stifled this ugly little thought as quickly as she could. She was going to trust Jared. That was what she'd decided to do in Victoria, and the fact that he wasn't home in the middle of the night in New York wasn't going to change her mind.

Swiftly Devon went into the bathroom, where she showered and put on a pretty nightgown to give herself courage, then she got into bed. Pulling the covers over her head so she wouldn't be so aware of the huge, empty house that surrounded her, she closed her eyes.

Within five minutes, she was asleep.

Devon woke from a dream in which she was maid-of-honor at a wedding. She replayed it in her mind, not sure whether to laugh or cry. Aunt Bessie was playing ragtime on the organ, and all Alicia's husbands were lined up as ushers. Devon was marrying Steve and Jared was marrying Lise, whose bouquet was a huge bundle of skunk cabbage. And then Steve dropped the ring, which landed in an empty champagne glass, shattering it into a thousand pieces.

Glass tinkled to the floor downstairs. A man's voice said something indistinguishable, then a door snapped shut and footsteps crossed the hardwood flooring. Devon sat up, her eyes widening with panic, her heartbeat almost deafening her. She hadn't dreamed that. No, that had been real. Someone was in the house. As quietly as she could, she picked up the phone beside the bed, dialled 911 and whispered, ''Burglar—hurry,'' when the woman answered. Then she slipped out of bed and glided over to the door. The small gold bolt was more decorative than useful. But the bureau beside the door was solid mahogany. She put her back to it, panic giving her strength, and shoved it in front of the door, wincing as it scraped across the floor.

Through the door she heard the sound of rough voices, then someone's shoulder crashed against the panels. Biting her lip to stop herself from screaming, she added her own weight to that of the bureau. Leaning back on it as hard as she could, she closed her eyes and prayed that the police would hurry.

Jared took a cab from the Vancouver airport. Thomas and Sally were still in Calgary; he'd told them to stay put because there was nothing they could do at the house. He didn't really know what he was doing back in Vancouver, unless it was obeying a deep, irrational need to be as close as possible to the last place Devon had been seen.

She hadn't used her credit card, hadn't made a plane or hotel reservation under her own name, hadn't been seen on the train going east. She'd taken a cab to the station and then she'd dropped out of sight.

The message was obvious. She didn't want to be found.

So why was he back here looking for her? And why did he feel as strung out as if he were about to fall flat on his face in the biggest deal of his whole career?

As clearly as if he were already there, he could picture the mansion overlooking the mountains and the bay. He'd ordered the furniture almost a year ago, sight unseen; the walls still cried out for paintings; the floors were bare of rugs. He'd never put any thought into the house, any of himself. Yet he'd dumped Devon there without a second thought, miles from her family and even more miles from Manhattan, because he'd had this vague idea of her making a home out of the house.

Without him. He hadn't even slept with her there.

I'm lonely, she'd said. I'm lonely for you, Jared. And he'd shrugged her words off, because he'd had more important matters on his mind.

The cab pulled up at a red light. She could be staying half a mile from the house, for all he knew. Or she could be out of the country. She must have a lot of overseas friends from all her travels.

He'd never bothered asking about her friends. He'd been too busy taking her to bed. Too busy making money.

Blame and discouragement sat like lead weights on his shoulders. Not to mention exhaustion: he hadn't had a proper night's sleep since Wallace had read him Devon's letter. Did you never truly value what you had until you'd lost it? Jared wondered, gazing out the window as the cab started to move again. Devon had fallen in love with him on their honeymoon. But had he noticed? No, sir. Not him. He'd been too worried about forgetting his own rules, about being totally out of control; he'd hated being at the mercy of a woman with sea-blue eyes and hair like silk. Her feelings hadn't entered into it. He'd had no room for them.

He'd been a self-centered bastard, he thought bitterly. And what if it was too late? Even if he found Devon, he couldn't force her to come back to him. She didn't want his money. And if she couldn't bring herself to trust him, they were done for.

He might not know much about marriage or feelings, but he'd finally figured that one out. She was right. Trust was basic.

The traffic was surprisingly heavy for so late at night. To Jared's overstrained imagination, it felt as though they were crawling along more slowly than he could walk. But why was he in a hurry? All that was waiting for him was an empty house, barren of clues to Devon's whereabouts.

He'd blown it. He, Jared Holt, head of Holt Incorporated, hadn't been able to hold onto his wife of less than two months. She'd run away from him, and she wasn't playing games. He knew Devon well enough for that.

His passionate, beautiful Devon.

Pain lanced through his chest. How could he have been so goddamned stupid? He was renowned for his quick intelligence, his instant grasp of any situation, his ability to make the right decision. But when it came to Devon, he'd behaved with as much subtlety as a four-year-old in a toy store.

The taxi was finally gathering speed along the boulevard by the golf course. Jared said through the connecting window, "Take the first turnoff after the clubhouse. It's the second driveway on the left."

They took the corner too fast, the tires screeching. Jared pulled out his wallet, checking the meter and extracting a bill. Then the cabbie said, "The house where all the police cars are? Looks like you got yourself a bit of trouble."

Jared glanced up. His heart gave an uncomfortable thump

as he heard the wail of sirens and saw three police cruisers parked in his driveway, the flashing red and blue lights casting surreal shadows over the clipped yews. He thrust the bill through the window, said, "Keep the change," and grabbed his bag. Then he was out of the cab and running toward the front door. A police officer stepped out from behind the nearest cruiser to intercept him. "Excuse me, sir, you can't go in there."

Jared said roughly, "It's my house—what's going on?"

"Couple of burglars, sir. We've apprehended two of them, but we're just checking in case there are more."

For the first time Jared noticed two men standing by one of the cruisers, both of them handcuffed. "They were in the house?"

"Yes, sir. Are you Jared Holt?"

Jared nodded. "The security system must have alerted you, right?"

"No, sir. The alarm was given by an occupant—"

Jared's heart gave another huge lurch. "No one's home. My wife's—away."

"I believe a woman gave the alarm, sir. Dialed 911."

"From this house? Are you sure?"

"Yes, sir. She—"

In cold terror, Jared snapped, "Where is she?"

"We're not quite sure yet, sir. We're about to—"

"For God's sake, man, don't just stand there, we've got to find her!" As he took two impetuous steps toward the house, the officer grabbed him by the elbow. Jared snarled, "You can come with me, or I'm going in alone. And heaven help anyone who gets in my way."

The officer, who looked about nineteen, yelled out some instructions to one of the other policemen. As Jared leaped up the front steps and burst through the front door, the young officer was at his heels. "Upstairs," Jared said tersely. "Did the woman leave her name?"

"No, sir."

It had to be Devon. It had to be. So where was she? As Jared took the big staircase two steps at a time, nightmare images crowded his brain. Devon raped. Knocked unconscious. Lying dead in a pool of blood.

Every cell in his body screamed out against this. She couldn't be dead. Not his vibrant, generous Devon. She couldn't be...he couldn't bear it.

He was the one who'd left her alone here.

The master bedroom was empty, the drawers pulled out just as he'd left them. No one had slept in the bed. Feeling his veins coagulate with ice, Jared shouted, "Devon? Are you up here? It's safe now—you can come out."

"Over there, sir."

Then Jared heard it, too: a scrabbling from one of the guest rooms, and then the voice he'd been frantic to hear: Devon's voice, weak with relief. "Jared? Is it really you?"

"The police are with me—open the door."

Wood scraped on wood. She said breathlessly, "It's so heavy, I'm not sure I can—there it goes." Then Jared heard the sound of the bolt being drawn, and the door opened.

She was wearing her blue silk robe over her nightgown; her eyes were huge, her face as pale as the white sheets on the bed behind her. Her knuckles were also white, where she was gripping the doorframe, gripping it as though she might fall down otherwise, Jared thought. He took three steps toward her and took her in his arms, pressing her to his chest, his whole body overwhelmed with gratitude and joy and some other emotion new to him, as powerful as the ocean tides and as sure of itself as the heat of the sun.

"Thank God you're safe," he said huskily.

She was trembling very lightly all over. As another officer joined the first one for a rapid search from room to room, Jared simply held Devon, certain that he held heaven in his arms. He'd been granted a reprieve, he thought. And this time there'd be no mistakes. He was going to do it right.

Against her hair, he said, "Get dressed—we'll go to a hotel."

"I hate this house," she muttered.

"I should never have left you here. Where are your clothes?"

She pushed back from his arms, not meeting his eyes. "In the room...I won't be a minute."

The next thirty minutes felt like forever to Jared. Apparently there'd only been the two burglars, neither of whom Jared or Devon had ever seen before. Devon answered the young officer's questions from the circle of Jared's arm, because he wasn't sure he was ever going to let go of her. Then the two of them were driven downtown in a police cruiser, to a luxury hotel belonging to one of Jared's worldwide chains. In the top floor suite, the bellboy put their luggage down and Jared tipped him. Finally the door closed and Jared was alone with his wife.

She was wearing overalls and a green sweater; she looked exhausted and deeply uncertain of herself, the soft light from the nearest lamp shadowing her cheekbones and lingering in her long blond hair. As always, her beauty infiltrated every nerve in Jared's body, as primal and profound as his relief that he'd found her and that she was safe. But now that they were alone, he had no idea what to say to her. What to say or what to do.

How long was it since he'd made love with her? It felt like forever; but although he longed to take her in his arms again, something stopped him. She was fiddling with the strap of her shoulder bag; she said so quietly that he had to strain to hear her, "Jared, why did you come back to the house tonight?"

"I was looking for you," he said bluntly.

Unsmiling, making no move to touch him, she said, "Why?"

She had, with her usual directness, gone right to the heart of the matter. He fumbled for the right words, the ones that would convince her never to run away again, and opted for the simple truth. "I had to. No choice."

"Because I've embarrassed you? Because you can't bear to lose—especially to a woman?" She raised her chin defiantly. "Aren't you supposed to be in San Francisco? On business?"

"Yes. But I had something much more important to do. Find my wife." Then Jared took a deep breath and said the words that had been forcing their way to the surface ever since Wallace had read her letter to him in Texas. The only words that counted. The true words. "I love you."

He heard his own voice speak them, those three small words he'd never thought he'd ever say to a woman, and watched shock freeze Devon's features. Shock, not joy.

She still didn't trust him. Worse, maybe she didn't love him anymore.

"It's true," he said, standing his ground, knowing he was fighting for his life, and that if he lost this battle then he himself was lost. "You had to run away for me to understand what you meant to me... I've never slept with Lise, Devon. Not once in all the months I've known her. She and I met up in Singapore two years ago, when she was on tour. That was when those photos were taken— you've got to believe me!"

"What do you think I'm doing in Vancouver?" Devon said. "Why do you think I came back?"

Jared shook his head like a man stunned. He was losing his grip, he thought. It hadn't even occurred to him to wonder. "My turn to ask why."

"I was having tea at The Empress—"

"How did you get to Victoria? Did you fly?"

"Took the bus. Changed my clothes at the train station." For the first time a faint smile lifted Devon's mouth. "Agent 007 had better look to his laurels, don't you think?"

"You really didn't want me to find you."

"Of course I didn't. Adultery's a horrible word. But while I was having tea I overheard a conversation that made me contrast you with Lise. I decided she was the one I shouldn't trust... But if you weren't with Lise, Jared, why wouldn't you take me to Singapore?"

"Because I didn't understand what loving a woman meant," he said, stepping closer and very gently stroking a strand of hair back from her face. "I never thought I'd fall in love, Devon, I've told you that. It wasn't in the cards. But ever since Wallace read your letter to me I've broken every rule in the book. Daniels finished off the rest of the board meeting in Texas, and Gregson's covering San Francisco for me. I'm finally learning how to delegate, in other words. And guess what? The world hasn't come to an end."

She was standing statue-still. He said, hearing desperation roughen his voice, "I love you, Devon. I want you to share my life—and that means all of it. Including the crises in Singapore and the board meetings in Texas." He took a deep breath, wondering what he'd do if she said no. "I'm supposed to open a new hotel in Australia next month—will you come with me?"

"You really do love me?" she asked in a small voice.

"That was what I was trying to tell you every time we went to bed...even though I didn't know it myself. But my body knew. We were making love, Devon, you were right." He smiled at her. "Yes, I love you. More than words can say...it might take the rest of my life to show you how much."

Tears filled her eyes, clinging to her lashes. "I'm not dreaming?"

And finally Jared did what he'd been needing to do ever since they'd walked into the hotel. He took her in his arms, holding her close, rediscovering with a shock of wonder her warmth and softness. "I'm real," he said huskily. "Dearest Devon, I love you so much."

Two tears spilled over. "I've come home, then," Devon said and lifted her face to his. "Home is with you, wherever you are. It's that simple."

He wiped the moisture from her cheekbone. "Don't cry, sweetheart."

"I'm so happy, that's why I'm crying." Her smile was brilliant, a rainbow through rain. "Don't you see? We love each other—so we have a real marriage. We're not trapped anymore, either one of us, we're free instead."

"You always were wiser than me," he said, and bent his head to kiss her. Then he took her by the hand and led her into the bedroom, where he undressed her in total silence, his hands not quite steady.

They made love with a slow and passionate intensity, every touch, every caress suffused with feeling. And when it was over Devon wept again, and Jared's throat was so tight he could only hold her and marvel at his happiness. "I love you," he whispered; now that he'd said it once, he was convinced he'd never be able to say it often enough.

"I feel so well loved, so safe," she murmured. "You know, Lise did us a favor in a way."

He gave a choked laugh. "I suppose she did. Shall we invite her to the christening?"

"Why not?" Devon pressed his hand to her belly. "Jared, our baby will be one of the lucky ones. Because its parents love each other."

"I knew what I was doing when I insisted we got married...I just went about it all the wrong way. Now that I

look back, I loved you from the first moment I saw you,"
he said. "Scowling at me in that hideous green suit."

She chuckled. "I thought you were the butler."

"You know what's so wonderful?" Jared added. "That
you love me for myself...not for my money."

"I love you because you're so stubborn and so sexy."

"Sexy?" he said innocently, running a hand down her
body to nestle between her thighs.

"Also insatiable—Jared, stop it!"

He leaned on one elbow, openly laughing at her. "You
really want me to stop?"

She moved her hips very suggestively. "I suppose we
do have to make up for lost time...do you know why else
I love you? Because you came looking for me."

"You did, too. You decided to trust me, and came
home." He hesitated. "I'd like to sell the Vancouver house,
Devon. Let's get a place in the country somewhere outside
New York. A real home, one we choose together."

"With the children in mind," she said, and wound her
arms around his neck.

"Sounds good to me," said Jared. "How many?"

"At least two," she said, her eyes dancing. "After all,
we have a duty to keep your father and my mother in grandchildren."

"Your first duty," Jared growled, nuzzling his lips to
her breast, "is to pay attention to what I'm doing."

"Oh, that's not a duty, Jared," Devon said. "That's a
pleasure. Trust me."

EPILOGUE

Six months later, standing in the warm midsummer sunshine that streamed through the window, Devon watched as Jared stooped to put Bruce Jared Holt back in the cradle. Jared's big hands were very gentle, and in the last few weeks he'd gotten over his initial fears that the baby would break if he as much as picked him up. Carefully Jared drew the covers up to the baby's chin, an expression on his face that made her melt inside.

Jared loved his son. She'd seen that from the very first time her husband had held the baby, only five minutes after the birth; the look on Jared's carved features that day, compounded of awe and joy and tenderness, had brought tears to her eyes.

She'd just fed the baby. His dark lashes wavered over his deep blue eyes, then closed altogether; his wisps of hair looked very black in contrast to the white coverlet. She bent to tuck it in at the foot of the carved wooden cradle, hearing the soft pad of bare feet come up behind her on the burnished pine flooring. Jared slid his hands around her waist.

"He looks fat and happy," Jared said.

"And utterly beautiful," she responded contentedly.

"Never as beautiful as his mother."

Devon turned in the circle of his arms. "But I haven't really got my figure back yet, and—"

Jared closed her mouth with his lips. A satisfactory interval later, he said huskily, "Darling Devon, you could be nine months pregnant with septuplets and I'd still think you were the most beautiful creature on earth—have you got that straight?"

183

Her six-weeks checkup had been just yesterday; while it had been sheer heaven to make love to Jared again in their big bed last night, Devon had still worried that he might not care for the inevitable alterations in her body. "Truly?" she said.

"Truly." He nuzzled her throat. "Come back to bed, and I'll do my best to prove it to you. Once again."

"We can't be too long—Benson and Alicia are arriving today."

Jared chuckled, smoothing the swell of Devon's hips under her silk gown. "It's only their third visit since Bruce was born."

"I don't know which one of them's worse—your father or my mother."

"Besotted, both of them." Jared looked around. "They like the house, too, of course."

"The house has nothing to do with it!"

"You like it, though, don't you, Devon?"

"I adore it," she said honestly.

They'd bought a restored eighteenth-century farmhouse on two hundred acres of rolling countryside only an hour from Manhattan on the interstate. The house came complete with barns and meadows and a network of horse trails; Rajah and Starlight were already in residence, gifts from Benson before Bruce had been born. The house was spacious, combining old-world charm with a sense of welcome that Devon had responded to from the first moment they'd walked in the door. She added, wrinkling her nose at her husband, "It's as different from the Vancouver place as it could be. And I've always wanted a fireplace in the bedroom."

"Even when you've got me?" he growled.

"Yep." She laced her hands around his neck, smiling into his dark eyes, so like his son's. "Did I tell you yet today that I love you?"

"You said you adored the house. But I don't recall you mentioning me."

"I adore you, too." Her eyes shining, she added softly, "Jared, I didn't know anyone could be as happy as I am now."

A muscle tightened in his jaw. With a humility new to him, he asked, "I really do make you happy?"

"Of course you do."

"No of course about it...for a long time I didn't."

"Oh, Jared, that's behind us now. Look at the changes we've made! A house we both love. A perfectly gorgeous son. And—" she gave him a saucy grin "—at last you've learned to delegate."

"Daniels in charge on the east coast, Gregson on the west, and Holt Incorporated, I hate to admit it, is flourishing east and west."

Devon laughed. "Not only that, but you've got the world's best lawyer working for you, too!"

"Of course I have."

Devon didn't just mean in terms of traveling on business with Jared, although certainly she'd done some of that in the last few months. More importantly, he was gradually sharing with her more and more of the complex decisions he made every day, and to her delight was consulting her frequently on points of international law, so much so that she was thinking of doing some post-graduate work once Bruce was a little older. She said, "I've become your wife in all ways. And I love it."

"We can talk about the takeover in Honolulu later," he said, stroking the ripe curve of her breast. "But right now I've got other things on my mind."

She widened her eyes innocently. "You always did know how to prioritize."

"It's one of the secrets of my success," Jared said, edging her toward the bed. "What time do the grandparents arrive?"

"For lunch."

"Then I've got two hours to convince you you're the most irresistible woman this side of the Appalachians."

"I should think you'll be able to manage that," Devon said, trembling from the intensity in his eyes.

"I'm going to do my best," Jared said.

To the satisfaction of both of them, he succeeded admirably. And if at lunchtime Devon had very rosy cheeks and Jared looked a man deeply in love and thoroughly satiated, Benson and Alicia were both too tactful and too excited about seeing baby Bruce to say a word.

HINTLTW

$ **Saving Money Has Never Been This Easy!** $

Just fill out and send in this form from any October, November and December 2002 books and we will send you a coupon booklet worth a total savings of $20.00 off future purchases of Harlequin and Silhouette books in 2003.

Yes! It's that easy!

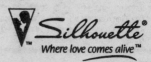

© 2002 Harlequin Enterprises Limited   PHQ402

International bestselling author

SANDRA MARTON

invites you to attend the

WEDDING *of the* YEAR

Glitz and glamour prevail in this volume
containing a trio of stories in which
three couples meet at a
high society wedding—and
soon find themselves
walking down the aisle!

Look for it in November 2002.

HARLEQUIN®
Makes any time special ®

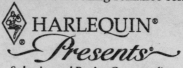

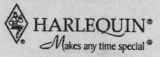